"Kissing me causes you grief?"

Cassy had to ask. She couldn't believe her ears. But in the close confines of the yacht, she couldn't have heard wrong.

"What's giving me grief is that kissing you isn't the only thing I want to do." Jon massaged the back of his neck. "I mean, usually I need to know a woman a long time before we—"

"Make love?"

"Hell, Cassy. Do you always have to be so blunt?" Jon jumped to his feet. "The point is, do you understand?"

"Sure. You're not interested in going to bed with me because we've just met." Her gaze unwavering, Cassy moistened her lips. "What do you intend to do about it?"

Jon drained his brandy glass and shuddered. "I'm not thinking clearly. Suppose you tell me."

Cassy set her snifter aside and rose. She stood so close they were almost touching. "Why don't we just try the kiss... and not worry about what comes later...?"

Kate Jenkins was shocked and amused when she read about the antics of the men—and women—at a local bachelor auction. The event got Kate thinking about what would happen if a man and woman participated under duress. The result is her third delightful Temptation, *The Reluctant Bachelor*.

Kate met her own "reluctant bachelor" at a Halloween masquerade ball, and this year marks the Houston couple's twentieth anniversary. There's no disguising love at first sight!

Books by Kate Jenkins
HARLEQUIN TEMPTATION
182–ON THE WILD SIDE
227–SUDDENLY, SUNSHINE

Don't miss any of our special offers. Write to us at the following address for information on our newest releases.

Harlequin Reader Service
901 Fuhrmann Blvd., P.O. Box 1397, Buffalo, NY 14240
Canadian address: P.O. Box 603,
Fort Erie, Ont. L2A 5X3

The Reluctant Bachelor
KATE JENKINS

Harlequin Books

TORONTO • NEW YORK • LONDON
AMSTERDAM • PARIS • SYDNEY • HAMBURG
STOCKHOLM • ATHENS • TOKYO • MILAN

Published October 1989

ISBN 0-373-25369-9

Copyright © 1989 by Linda Jenkins-Nutting. All rights reserved.
Except for use in any review, the reproduction or utilization
of this work in whole or in part in any form by any electronic,
mechanical or other means, now known or hereafter invented,
including xerography, photocopying and recording,
or in any information storage or retrieval system, is forbidden without
the permission of the publisher, Harlequin Enterprises Limited,
225 Duncan Mill Road, Don Mills, Ontario, Canada M3B 3K9.

All the characters in this book have no existence outside the
imagination of the author and have no relation whatsoever to
anyone bearing the same name or names. They are not even
distantly inspired by any individual known or unknown to the
author, and all incidents are pure invention.

® are Trademarks registered in the United States Patent and
Trademark Office and in other countries.

Printed in U.S.A.

1

CASSY LAURENS TOOK ONE LOOK at Bachelor Number Seven and revised her plan for the evening. Seven had just become her lucky number.

She shivered and told herself it was because the elegant hotel ballroom was frigid enough to rival Minnesota in January. But it was August in Houston, and her red cotton blouse clung to her back, a clammy reminder of the four-hour trip in a car with no air conditioning. Cassy had been to east Texas recruiting volunteers for her current project and would have preferred to stay there. At least the piney woods provided a shady illusion of coolness. Here the freeways simply sweltered and buckled from stress and heat.

But a promise was a promise.

Cassy tucked the glossy auction program under one arm while she searched for her glasses in her small shoulder bag. After finding only a wallet, checkbook, comb and lip gloss, she patted the pockets of her rumpled khaki suit. Nothing in there but keys. No matter how many pairs she bought, the glasses vanished with alarming frequency. Fortunately she only needed the dime-store magnifiers for reading, but misplacing them so often was an annoying, wasteful habit. Above everything, Cassy hated squandering money.

Sighing in disgust, she held the program at arm's length and closed one gray eye in order to focus.

"Uh-oh. Lost your cheaters again, I see," her best friend, Meredith Winslow, teased, tugging Cassy's fraying ash-brown braid. "I'm glad you made it. Knowing this is the last place you want to be, I half expected you to send a check and claim you'd fallen victim to dengue fever."

Cassy rolled her eyes. Meredith, a high school drama coach, tended to be overly dramatic. Almost six feet of height and a glorious mane of red hair further enhanced her stunning presence. "I merely said that I thought bachelor auctions were last year's craze." She had to shout to be heard over the intrusive rock music.

"And I told you that the Hunger Coalition isn't one of the movers and shakers' pet causes. We're the drudges, trying to scrounge every dollar we can for food. They may be passé, but these prime beef sales bring in a lot of money. That's all we care about."

A blond hunk in a white tuxedo swaggered by, stopping only long enough to favor them with a high-wattage smile. "Be still my beating heart," Meredith gasped, patting her chest in a predictable response. "Cass, be a pal. Buy that one and donate him to me. I'm in dire need of whatever Dream Date he's offering."

Cassy tipped her head and watched the departing bachelor, appearing to consider his merits before nodding. "A walking tribute to orthodontia, tanning parlors and exercise equipment," she commented dryly. "Sorry, I've already decided which one I'm going to buy." She pointed toward the cluster of people standing beneath a tiered, mistletoe-draped chandelier. Surrounded by a fawning harem, the lone male looked distinctly uncomfortable. Several women were bold enough to try using the mistletoe to their advantage, but Number Seven had more feints than Muhammad Ali in his prime. "Him."

"Ah, yes. I see." From a distance Meredith examined the candidate with slow thoroughness. Then she said cryptically, "Be careful with that one, my friend."

"Why?" Cassy asked, puzzled because Meri constantly pestered her to take more interest in the opposite sex. Now that she had, Meri was urging caution.

"Surely you've heard about those touch-me-not types," Meredith said with a lascivious wink. "Below the surface they're supposed to be seething with volcanic passion, waiting to erupt."

Cassy shivered again, and this time she recognized it for what it was—the thrill of anticipation. "Does that mean you approve of my choice?"

"Why, of course, dah-ling. He looks delectable."

Cassy grinned. "You're too diplomatic. He looks like he has an excruciating toothache," she said bluntly. "Those women may be camouflaged in silk and good jewelry, but they're swarming like piranhas in a feeding frenzy." She studied the tall, dark-haired man, not just sympathizing but actually feeling his desperate need to escape. "That's why I have to rescue him."

"Then let's check to see whom you'll be saving," Meredith suggested, snatching Cassy's program and riffling pages to find the proper entry. "Jonathan Manning, thirty-four, bachelor of business administration from Texas A&M, co-owner of Atlantis Properties, developers of luxury resorts in North America and the Caribbean—" Her monologue came to an abrupt halt, and she shook Cassy's arm. "Do you realize he's Pat Gibson's partner?" She touched her bosom in a theatrical pose. "Oh, this is sooo rich! Pat's a coalition volunteer, too, and he must have conned his partner into being an auctionee, just like I coerced you into being a bidder. The symbolism is positively cosmic!" She read further.

Cassy wasn't interested in any of the superficial hype. She didn't need to know that he was six feet tall and weighed 175. Or that he played pick-up basketball at a city recreational center for exercise. She already knew the only thing that was important about Jonathan Manning.

He was her fate.

She wasn't gifted with second sight, or at least she hadn't been in the past. This was different. There was no logical explanation for it, yet somehow she *knew*. She'd stepped into the noisy, overflowing ballroom, and her eyes had instantly zeroed in on one man. Without knowing his name or anything else about him, Cassy had rearranged her future to include him. She hadn't been looking for a man, but she was pragmatic enough to accept that Jonathan Manning wasn't one of life's options. She touched her stomach, discovering that her insides weren't nearly so tranquil as her exterior.

"N.B.M.—that's never been married," Meredith informed Cassy in her best schoolteacher's voice. Then she whispered loudly, "Translate—no ex-wives, no alimony, no child support. A real bonus in this day and age. And listen to this. His Dream Date is a week with him—separate rooms—at the Atlantis resort on Aruba. To die for! Why can't I find a guy like this in real life?"

Cassy was in the middle of suggesting that Meredith enjoyed flirting with men in general too much to concentrate on one in particular, when she was interrupted. The mistress of ceremonies took the stage and accepted a microphone. "Sorry, ladies, but preview time is up. You have to stop fondling the merchandise." Cassy groaned along with everyone else, but not because she wanted the hands-on happy hour to last longer. Meredith giggled.

Cassy sent her a stern look. "I can't help it. To me, buying another person's company, even to benefit a good cause, seems vaguely... sordid. Demeaning. Only one step up from being in a strip joint when the cops raid it."

Meredith laughed harder, steering her to one of the long linen-covered tables arranged for bidders.

The amplified female voice exhorted, "Now it's time to get those bids up there as high as your estrogen levels."

"Oh, brother. I'll bet she spent months thinking up that line." With the bidding about to start, Cassy felt strangely tense. She compensated by trying to sound droll.

The first two candidates, full of confidence, strutted down the runway to cheers and wolf whistles. One brought a thousand dollars, the other, fourteen hundred. A third jerked and gyrated like a marionette with tangled strings and pushed his price a few hundred higher. The affluent crowd was eating up the men's antics and screaming for more.

Cassy kept glancing at her watch, wishing they would cut the cutesy chatter and get done with the first six bachelors. She'd already stayed longer than originally planned and could only spare a few more minutes. Everything important in her life seemed to be happening at once, and it occurred to her that meeting Jonathan Manning would have been much more convenient a few months from now.

Backstage Jon leaned against a wall, hands crammed in his pockets. He knew what a condemned man must feel like, sweating while he waited for the executioner to put him out of his misery. Friendship be damned! Why had he agreed to be part of this farce? While awaiting his fate, Jon composed a long list of diabolical schemes to pay back his partner. Wasted effort, he supposed, since he probably wouldn't survive to exact revenge. Damn Pat! He'd known just what button to punch.

Jon's stomach felt as if a nest of snakes had taken up residence. His palms itched and his collar must have shrunk two sizes since he arrived. He reached up to unbutton it and loosen the knot of his tie. If he didn't relieve some of the pressure, he'd be hyperventilating.

Jon had a reputation for being unflappable under pressure. He valued that, cultivated it. But tonight his composure was completely shot because some woman with an evening to spare and bucks to blow was going to insinuate herself into his life, no matter how fleetingly.

He was nothing more than a slave on the auction block, and the woman with the most money could buy him. He resented the implications, the loss of control, the vulnerability.

"Oh, hell!" he muttered, jerking off his coat and flinging it onto a nearby chair.

"Hey, man, lighten up. This is supposed to be a fun gig," one of the other victims called to him.

The Reluctant Bachelor 11

Some fun, Jon thought glumly. There must be worse punishments than enduring this humiliation and having to spend a week with a stranger. But right now he couldn't think of a more dismal prospect.

He stared disbelievingly as Bachelor Number Six stripped off his shirt, dropped to the floor and began a vigorous set of push-ups. After the workout, he adjusted his indecently tight jeans and started oiling his bare chest. The sweet smell of coconut was almost as sickening as the cloying scent of perfume that had swamped him during the cocktail hour. He longed for one good breath of fresh air.

Seeing Jon's grimace, the muscle man explained, "A good pump fills your chest and arms with blood." He chugged a glass of wine and added, "If I've gone without water for a couple of days, my veins stick out. The wine makes me look vascular, really ripped. That's important if I want to bring top dollar. You ought to see for yourself."

Under other circumstances, Jon might have tried to act impressed. As it was, he simply stared at the vain peacock as if he were some alien life-form and waited his turn.

When the time came, he straightened his spine and marched out for the obligatory runway tour. With spotlights blinding him, he couldn't make out any of the faces below him, which was just as well. But he could hear the chant, "Strip, strip." That exhibitionist before him had whetted their appetite for skin. Too bad. This was as good as they were going to get.

The predatory energy was tangible enough to suffocate him, but the end was in sight. Only the actual bidding remained, followed by a dreaded, and if he had anything to say about it, brief, meeting with the winner before he could get out of there. After that it ought to be fairly easy to contrive some means of avoiding the trip. Women who fancied this sort of fun probably viewed buying men as a novel way to relieve boredom. No way was he going to flit off to Aruba with some rich dilettante.

"So tell us, Jonathan, what did you do to get ready for this evening?" The mistress of ceremonies, an attractive but rapacious-looking woman, was ogling him so lewdly that he had the urge to check his fly.

Instead, he forced her to meet his eyes, then faced the audience with a deadpan expression. "I put on a clean shirt and made sure my socks matched."

At least some of them had a sense of humor, he thought, listening to the scattered laughter.

The emcee winked at him, as if they shared a secret, then growled into the mike. "Well, ladies, you can see that he looks lean and mean. But let me tell you, up close, these gorgeous green eyes are full of naughty promises." She ran one red-taloned hand possessively over Jon's chest before he could step back. "All this splendid masculinity can be yours for the taming. What am I bid for Number Seven?"

Without a second's hesitation, a feminine voice called out clearly, decisively, "Ten thousand dollars."

Jon didn't echo the collective gasp or the buzz of comments that rose from the audience. He was too astonished to make a sound and too stunned to move after hearing the extravagant bid. Finally the emcee whispered that he'd better get off the stage and grab the lady who was so "hot" for his company. Her simpering suggestiveness snapped him from his daze in a hurry.

He hated admitting it, but he was curious about the woman who'd pay so much money for him.

Cassy was on her feet, poised for a quick getaway the instant she announced her bid. By the time the shocked crowd got around to speculating on her identity, she had disappeared out the door, and Meredith was scurrying to catch up with her.

She hurriedly dropped off the check she'd already filled out and was calculating her driving time to the airport. She had to go—it was essential. But Cassy was torn. She wanted to meet Jonathan, to begin getting acquainted. "Not tonight," she whispered to herself regretfully.

She had her '71 Chrysler Imperial fired up and in Drive when Meredith wrestled open the passenger door. "Got a plane to meet." Cassy's terse explanation was paired with a dismissing flick of her hand. Ignoring that, her friend leaped inside. "Don't say I didn't warn you," Cassy said as she stomped on the accelerator. They roared out of the hotel parking lot accompanied by a smoky-blue aura and the clatter of a loose tail pipe.

"For pity's sake, Cass. You're crazy to run off and leave that divine man behind."

"I told you. I've got to get to Hobby, and fast." She sent all four power windows creaking down.

Muggy air gusted through Meredith's long hair, demolishing her stylish upsweep. "You didn't tell me you're going out of town," she said, digging for the scarf she always kept in Cassy's glove compartment.

"I'm not. I'm meeting Robert Huntington, and I don't think he's the type to give a minute's grace if I'm late."

She shot past a slow-moving car and cut across two lanes of congested Galleria area traffic.

"Isn't he that corporate type you've been trying to contact for months?"

"Yep, and after months of not being able to schedule an appointment or even speak to him on the phone, he suddenly agreed to meet with me for a few minutes between flights." The man and his company would be invaluable allies if she could convince him to support her medical-assistance program. She needed his help badly. "This is probably my one chance to sell him on the idea of a volunteer-staffed health-care plan in Honduras."

"I know that's the most important thing in your life right now," Meri said sympathetically, "and how hard you've worked to put it together. But where does that leave Jonathan Manning? You did pay an exorbitant amount of money for him, Cass. Aren't you even going to meet him?"

"As soon as possible, Meri. And every chance I get from now on."

Meredith glanced at the dashboard once they got on the Loop, but didn't comment that Cassy was exceeding the speed limit by nearly twenty miles an hour. "This doesn't sound like the same person who planned to clear out as soon as she bought the first bachelor, then donated him back to be reauctioned."

"That was before I saw Jonathan Manning and was swept away."

"That sounds more like something I'd do."

"You mean falling in love impulsively is your exclusive domain?" Cassy asked with tolerant amusement.

"'Falling in love'?" Meredith yelped. "Surely I didn't hear you correctly."

The old Chrysler sputtered and Cassy reacted with a familiar routine. She shoved the gear lever into Neutral and raced the engine. The car backfired once before settling back into its steady, droning rhythm.

Meredith pursed her lips. Cassy didn't know whether it was distaste for the car's performance or disbelief over her surprising declaration. "Don't worry about it, Meri," she soothed. "I have everything under control."

"Then heaven help Jonathan Manning," Meredith murmured under her breath. "He doesn't stand a chance."

Cassy smiled serenely and added, "Neither of us does."

"WHAT DO YOU MEAN you have no intention of going on our Dream Date?"

It had been three days since the auction, and Cassy had started to wonder if Jonathan would make the effort to track her down. Her airport meeting with the corporate president had turned out better than she'd hoped. He'd not only pledged financial backing, but he'd agreed to share some of his employees' time and expertise. But the minute she'd obtained his commitment, Cassy's thoughts had jumped to Jonathan.

She had wanted to call him right then to explain why she'd disappeared so abruptly and arrange a time to get together. But an inner voice counseled that she should let him take the initiative.

And he had. She just hadn't counted on the undisguised hostility she heard in his voice. "Let's see, how can I simplify?" Cassy hoped he didn't think she was playing hard to get. It had never been her plan to go on the Dream Date. Even her unexpected interest in Jonathan didn't change that. "I am not going to Aruba with you."

She heard him draw an exasperated breath. "You paid a lot for that trip...Charlotte Cassidy," he tacked on smugly.

Cassy coiled the phone cord around her little finger and smiled. He'd done some crafty detective work to discover what the initials C.C. on her check stood for. "Most people call me Cassy. And I paid that money to the Hunger Coalition for food. The auction and the trip had nothing to do with it."

He considered that for a few seconds before pouncing on the flaw in her explanation. "In that case, why did you bother coming? You could have accomplished the same thing with a contribution."

But then I wouldn't have seen you. "It's a long story, and I won't bore you with details. You looked miserable and obviously weren't enjoying yourself any more than I was. I figure we were both there for similar reasons."

"You went as a favor to a friend?" he asked warily, as if he couldn't quite believe it. Without confirming his guess, she allowed him time to reflect. At last he said, "I would have thought you'd want to be sure you got a few kicks out of the deal. After all, isn't that what you spent your daddy's hard-earned money on?"

Cassy sank into a comfortable old chintz-covered chair, reeling from the accusation. No wonder he'd sounded so antagonistic when she answered the phone. He wasn't the first person to assume she was a pampered and profligate rich bitch, though none of those terms described her. Except rich. She was that. Technically. But she didn't make a career of it. Of course, he had no way of knowing that.

"Jonathan, you're a very attractive man, which I'm sure you know." Cassy had sneaked a close-up with Meredith's opera glasses. She'd been overwhelmed when that one quick glance sent her heart racing wildly, much as it was now. "But character analysis isn't your forte. Best leave that to someone who knows me better."

"Wait a minute. I didn't—"

"Look at it this way. I'm sparing you from a trip that you clearly don't want to take. You ought to thank me for letting you off the hook." Defensiveness made her sound testy. Not the best way to change his opinion of her, but she couldn't help herself. "I don't want to seem rude, but I really have to run. You've caught me in the middle of something important." Again, she was almost late, this time for an orientation session with a group of nurses who'd signed on to go to Honduras.

Cassy broke the connection gently and imagined Jonathan Manning slamming down his receiver with a comment that was certifiably rude.

"I HOPE THAT WASN'T ONE of our financial backers," Pat Gibson remarked from the open doorway of Jon's office.

Jon didn't bother to answer. He was too busy glowering at the still-vibrating phone. He rarely swore and almost never lost his cool. He'd done a lot of both since getting involved in that accursed bachelor auction. "It's all your fault," he grumbled, pinning his partner with an intimidating stare. "Then you have the nerve to skip town."

"Whoa! I didn't exactly sneak out in the dead of night," Pat said, throwing his hands up in protest. "We are in the middle of a construction project, you know." He eased his lanky frame into one of the plush burgundy chairs across from Jon's desk and grinned sheepishly. "It's a rotten job, having to spend summer in the Colorado Rockies, but somebody's got to do it."

In lieu of another oath, Jon made an unintelligible sound deep in his throat. He was overreacting. He knew it. But damned if he could stop. He was feeling even more agitated now that he had a voice to go along with his vivid image of Charlotte Cassidy Laurens. It was a nice voice—soft, lyrical, almost silvery to his ear. It annoyed him that he liked anything at all about the elusive lady, because he knew the type. Spoiled, drowning in money, she had bought him with the same casual disregard she'd show any other trinket.

Now she was trying to brush him aside just as nonchalantly. It wasn't going to work.

"What's going on?" Pat demanded. "If this is my fault don't I deserve to know the nature of my offense?"

"I'll give you a hint," Jon said, springing out of his chair to pace, another atypical sign of restlessness. "If you ever need a human sacrifice for another bachelor auction, I'm permanently unavailable."

"Hey, buddy, I'm sorry," Pat apologized. "Guess you got stuck with a real dog, huh?" He scratched his head and looked contrite. "You know I'd never have imposed on our friendship if this was something I could do myself."

Jon stopped his prowling and almost smiled. Pat had used his marriage as the ploy to get Jon signed up for the auction, and it had worked. "Christie is a real sweetheart about all the traveling you have to do," he said, referring to Pat's very tolerant wife. "However, I think she'd draw the line at your taking a date to Aruba for a week." He'd often felt guilty that happily married Pat had to be gone so often while he, being unattached, handled things on the home front. But that was the reality of their business.

Pat laughed. "Yeah, she's pretty old-fashioned when it comes to stuff like that." He studied the calluses on his palms. "Just how bad is this woman, partner?"

It was Jon's turn to laugh, but there was no real humor in the sound. "That's just it. I have no idea. Rather than hang around and introduce herself, she disappeared. That is, she skipped after paying ten thousand dollars for me."

Pat whistled and shook his head. "I think the most anybody's ever brought before is about twenty-five hundred. Do you suppose she's playing a game, figuring for that kind of bread you should do a little chasing?"

"I thought so at first. These rich dolls have some strange ideas about manipulating people." Jon related how he'd coaxed and wheedled to no avail, finally resorting to charm so the cashier would let him look at the check. "Even that had only her initials and last name. No address or phone number. You wouldn't believe the arm-twisting I had to do to get her full name and unlisted phone number."

"Why did you bother?" Pat asked quietly, a question Jon had posed to himself more than once. "I mean, if she didn't follow the rules, theoretically you're free. You can't be expected to find a woman who goes to extreme lengths to cover her trail." His palm smacked against his forehead. "Uh-oh. The check bounced, right?"

"Hardly." Again Jon wished he'd never agreed to Pat's appeal for help. He could handle business crises with no hassle. In his personal life, he preferred tranquility. "Unlike most of us, I doubt if Charlotte Cassidy Laurens has ever had to worry about a hot check in her life."

"Cassy Laurens bought you?" Pat slapped his leg and guffawed. "I suspect the fine hand of Meredith Winslow in this. That meddling redhead could sell air conditioners in Lapland. So she finally got to Cassy."

"You know her?"

"Sure do. Met her over a year ago, when she first moved to Houston. Cassy's a nice lady."

"Nice," Jon said disparagingly, when he really wanted to ask what the woman in question looked like, where she lived, why Pat liked her.

"Nice," Pat reaffirmed, "in the best sense of the word. Cassy's a straight shooter, Jon. If she didn't leave her name or number, then she didn't want to hear from you. As I said before, you've fulfilled your obligation." His expression perplexed, he asked, "Why don't you leave it alone?"

"Well, Pat, that's the hell of it. I know it's crazy, but somehow I have to meet her. I won't rest until I do."

AS HE JOCKEYED for Friday afternoon rush hour space, Jon recalled the conversation he'd had with his partner. He and Pat had finally dreamed up a strategy for getting Cassy to see him. She'd made it clear she had no interest in his trip to Aruba, so it seemed useless to ask her for a regular date, as he might have done with anyone else. But Cassy Laurens had nothing in common with the women who usually appealed to him.

It had taken almost two weeks to reach her a second time on the phone. She no doubt needed a social secretary to keep up with her engagements. He had an unpleasant vision of her holding court in a River Oaks mansion, mingling with the common folk only on those rare occasions when charity deemed it necessary.

Like this afternoon. When Jon had proposed donating the value of their Aruba trip back to the Hunger Coalition, he'd insisted on her signing a release. Evidently she hadn't seen through that transparent ruse, because she'd consented to see him. His hand tightened on the wheel as he recalled their last conversation. She had suggested the time and place for this meeting, and he'd agreed with an eagerness he regretted at once. But it was as if he'd had no choice.

So far Cassy Laurens had called all the shots, and Jon wasn't comfortable with that realization. He wondered at this compulsion to see her in person. In the beginning he had simply wanted to give her a piece of his mind. Now he wasn't so sure. He only knew that he couldn't wait to come face-to-face with the lady.

Spotting the shabby Heights area cantina that she had selected, Jon's mouth turned down. Had she chosen it because she considered meeting him akin to going slumming? He scanned the parking lot for a status car. But all the vehicles looked as dusty and run-down as the unpaved expanse surrounding the café. Maybe a chauffeured Rolls had dropped her off and retreated to a more desirable part of town. He parked his black BMW at a safe distance from the other cars and activated its alarm system.

He stared down at his cordovan loafers as he crossed the lot, stirring up miniature dust devils that settled back onto the polished leather. Couldn't she have been predictable and picked a trendy restaurant, as he'd expected?

The smell of tortillas greeted him as he stepped inside, out of the bright afternoon sun. Jon checked out the few patrons while his eyes adjusted to the dim interior. Obviously she wasn't here yet. He should have known she'd keep him waiting. Her type would. He glanced up at a Dr. Pepper clock hanging crookedly on the cinder block wall. He was two minutes late for their five-thirty appointment. He'd give her until six, then take off. There was a limit to his forbearance.

One of the waitresses was eyeing Jon curiously. He guessed not many of their clientele showed up wearing suits and ties. Wait until they got a look at Cassy Laurens. She'd probably make an entrance trailing chiffon and dripping diamonds.

Finally, seeing that he wasn't going to seat himself, the waitress asked if she could help. He explained who he was supposed to be meeting, and before he finished, she gestured to a small round table in the corner.

"You must be mistaken," he said, frowning.

"Oh, no, sir," she assured him with a heavy accent. "That's Cassy, all right. She comes here all the time."

"She does? But I thought—"

"Don't you recognize the man with her, either?"

From the pitying tone of her voice, Jon figured he'd committed a major offense. He shrugged, waiting for the waitress to enlighten him.

"That's the Boise Bonebreaker, the famous wrestler. You must have seen him on TV."

"Mmm," he murmured noncommittally. Jon had never watched that pseudosport in his life. Until now.

Across the room Cassy Laurens was arm wrestling with a skinheaded, tattooed bruiser who was twice her size. And she was laughing with such delight that for a moment Jon could believe she had never enjoyed anything more.

2

SHE SPELLED TROUBLE, though not the kind he had first envisioned. Jon didn't know how he could be so positive, but he didn't question it. He only knew that he needed to find out more about the woman whose enchanting bell-like laughter drew him inexorably to her.

Far removed from the haughty sophisticate he had expected, Cassy looked awfully young and much too fragile to engage in hand-to-hand combat with any man. Especially not a tough, battle-scarred one whose yellow tank top showed off arms the size of tree trunks. He could crush her with one of his monster paws and not even feel the exertion. A fleeting image of himself rescuing her flickered across Jon's imagination, and he blinked to dispel it. Cassy Laurens did not need protection, or anything else, from him.

Advancing slowly over the uneven, faded linoleum, Jon heard Bonebreaker's guttural instruction. "Come on, girl. Try harder. Let me feel some muscle. Concentrate, Cassy, or your opponent will grind you into mincemeat."

Cassy's brow furrowed, her lips tightened, and with arms quivering, she put more power into her attack. Jon couldn't tell if she did it to placate the giant or if she responded to his taunt out of sheer competitiveness. Whatever, she was giving it her best effort, and the mountainlike man looked pleased. A wide grin split his battered face, revealing a gap between both his upper and lower front teeth.

The advantage seesawed back and forth several times before the wrestler allowed Cassy to force his arm down and pin it to the table. She thrust her fists high in a victory sign and laughed again. Then she looked up.

Jon stopped in his tracks the instant she saw him. Gazing into her gray eyes—clear, direct and shaded with just the tiniest hint of challenge—he changed his opinion of her yet again. Neither socialite nor ingenue, this woman stood at once, making no attempt to mask a very straightforward evaluation of him, even as she welcomed him with a smile. In spite of all his internal warnings, Jon was intrigued.

"Hello, Jonathan." Her voice sounded lower, huskier than it had on the phone, and it stroked over his nerve endings like a midnight whisper. He hesitated a second, flexing his fingers before taking the hand she offered. It was as silky as her voice. And just as evocative.

"Cassy," he said, striving for cool indifference and not quite making it. Maybe he should try humor. At the end of their last conversation, he'd asked how he would recognize her at the restaurant. Cassy had told him to wear matching socks, and she would recognize him. "Want to check my socks?"

Cassy's gaze dipped to his feet, then back up almost as quickly. Her smile deepened. Jonathan had apparently overcome his early resentment enough to joke with her. "Nope. Don't forget I had the advantage of seeing you onstage." Energized by a powerful surge of feminine awareness, she knew now that the binoculars had not done him justice.

Up close he seemed taller, whippet slim, vibrant with energy. Masculine. Cassy's palm slid away from his, and she inserted it into the pocket of her full, red cotton skirt. What she really wanted to do was rub it over the day-end shadow stubbling his lean jawline, sink her fingers into his coffee-brown hair and...

As if he read her thoughts, the Boise Bonebreaker made a growllike noise. "Oh, Herbert, I'm sorry," she apologized before introducing the two men. When Jonathan's teeth clenched, Cassy figured the wrestler had lived up to his ring name with a bruising handshake. Poor Herbert, always trying to defend her against men with dishonorable intentions.

"If you'll excuse us, Cassy and I have some business to discuss," Jonathan said, being excessively polite to the forbidding hulk. Her massive protector didn't move except to ripple the sinuous scarlet serpent branded on his left biceps. "I only want to talk to her." No response. He tried another dismissal tactic. "I can assure you I'm harmless."

Cassy knew that her self-appointed guardian wouldn't give up without some sign from her. When she patted his bald pate, as shiny as a newly minted silver dollar, he moved away, but only far enough to set up surveillance in a nearby booth.

"Does your paid muscle accompany you everywhere?"

Cassy grinned at the forced casualness of his question. "Herbert would be insulted by the suggestion that he'd accept money for being chivalrous. He believes single women need chaperones more now than they did several centuries ago." She neglected to add that the wrestler resorted to violence only for the benefit of his cheering fans. "He's really quaint and gallant, in his own way."

Jonathan cast a sidelong glance at the subject in question and shook his head, as if it were impossible to reconcile courtliness with the man's unorthodox appearance. After he muttered something about Bonebreaker being a more suitable name than Herbert, Cassy decided to change the subject.

She sat down, sending him a silent invitation to do the same. "So tell me, how did you get my name and unlisted phone number?"

"Trust me," he said with a grimace, "you don't want to know. I'm pretty sure it wasn't legal."

How revealing. Instinct told her that Jonathan Manning rarely had to employ such drastic measures in pursuit of a woman. Cassy looked away for a moment to control her satisfied smile.

"And I know it's going to cost me," he went on, drumming his fingers against the dull beige Formica tabletop.

She could tell he was still doubting whether he'd done the right thing. "Goodness, I hope you didn't make any reckless promises that you're already regretting."

His head jerked up. His stormy green eyes bored into hers, holding them captive for breathless seconds. "I never do anything recklessly, Cassy. Never!"

She let out a thin trail of air over her dry lips. She'd never heard more vehemence packed into a single statement. She had a feeling that her jest touched something very basic in Jonathan's character, something she needed to take seriously. She smiled her gratitude to the waitress who bustled up to take their drink order. After Jonathan requested a Mexican brand of beer, the young woman winked at Cassy and enumerated his manly virtues in rapid-fire Spanish.

Feeling not at all virtuous and being equally fluent, Cassy agreed and added a few of her own observations along with her order for plain water and lime.

"Like most native Texans, I have a passable command of Spanish," Jonathan said, assessing her through narrowed lids. "You have a northern accent, yet speak like you were born south of the Rio Grande. Come on, Cassy. Confess. Where did you learn bedroom language?"

"You understood?" She fought to keep the heat in her cheeks from showing. At the auction she'd observed that he shied away from voracious women, and she'd just been fairly specific in her appreciation.

"Not everything." His grin cut off her relieved sigh. "Enough to know that both of us should probably be blushing."

With a determined tilt of her chin, Cassy ignored her blunder. "My accent is pure Minnesotan. As for the Spanish, if two years in high school, a minor in college, four years as a Peace Corps volunteer in Latin America followed by another two as a language instructor didn't teach me almost everything there was to learn, then I ought to be stood up against a wall and shot."

"You've done all that?"

He didn't have to sound quite so amazed, she thought crossly. Then she remembered that Jonathan had more than one misguided notion about her. "Guar-an-teed," she drawled in her best Texas twang. "Surprised?"

"Yes," he admitted with a small frown, "I guess I am." His large, strong-looking hands curled around the red-

and-white can of Tecate the waitress placed in front of him. "Are there going to be more of these little bombshells, Charlotte Cassidy?"

"Yes, Jonathan. I'm afraid so."

He picked up the lime, bit into it, then completed the ritual with several healthy swallows of beer. His silence attested to the careful consideration he gave his next words. "Normally, I don't like surprises. I prefer things to be predictable. But it looks like I'll have to make an exception in your case." He shook his head several times before looking at her. "I don't seem to have any choice," he added with quiet resignation.

Nor did she, Cassy thought. But she could imagine Jonathan's reaction if she told him she'd taken one look at him and decided he was the man for her. She sensed that caution came naturally to him and knew he wasn't ready to hear words like *fate*.

"How old are you, Cassy?"

"Almost twenty-nine," she answered, thinking ahead to her trip to Minnesota for the birthday celebration. Judging from his doubtful look, her age didn't compute. She was used to that. "I imagine the pigtail fooled you into thinking I'm younger."

"I'd have guessed twenty, twenty-two at the most. Much too young for me." Right away he seemed appalled by his candor.

"When, in fact—"

"I'm only five years older. Just about right." After that admission, he really looked chagrined.

Cassy noted Jonathan's visible relief when deliverance from his impulsive remark arrived in the form of Mother Divine. Palmist, card reader and, by virtue of heredity and family pressure, part-time insurance executive, she swooped down to hover over them like a graceful, gardenia-scented cloud. Her brilliant blue embroidered shift cleverly matched the color of her eyes, in addition to concealing a figure that had opted for peaceful coexistence with carbohydrates.

Jonathan started to rise, but Mother checked the show of manners by pushing him back down into his tacky, peeling chair.

"Lit-tle Charlotte," she intoned, eyes half-closed to approximate a trancelike state. "The vibrations are exceedingly strong." She let one palm flutter down to settle on Cassy's shoulder, the other on Jonathan's. "Yes, yes. This will not be gainsaid."

Mother Divine was the only person Cassy knew who could get by with using such a pretentious word, and even then it was a close call. Maybe that three-inch-wide swath of white bisecting her waist-length jet hair imparted a certain air of credibility despite the affected way of speaking.

"This is Jonathan Manning," Cassy said, stifling a laugh when she saw him evaluating Mother through suspicious eyes.

"But of course," the middle-aged woman agreed, as if she had long ago presaged his identity. When she seized Jonathan's hand and clasped it between both of hers, her ring glittered. It was the stunning blue of a robin's egg and almost as large. She bowed her head, and after a fraught silence, reversed her sandwiched palms, revealing another gaudy gem, this one the variant pink and green shades of a watermelon.

Their part-time prophetess lapsed into a high-pitched hum, and that was clearly the last straw for Jonathan. Scowling fiercely, he struggled to reclaim his hand, but

Mother froze him with the brusque command, "Stop fighting what none save the universal forces can control. Only then will you find that which you seek."

A flush crept upward from his starched white collar, and Jonathan squirmed, his discomfort telegraphed by the crackling red plastic chair. Cassy's amusement faded when she read the tacit appeal in his eyes. He seemed to be signaling her to come up with an exit line.

"It's been great seeing you, Helen," she said in a chatty tone, using the woman's given name to neutralize the mystique factor. "But we were just on our way out."

"You can't leave yet," the seer protested, manipulating Jonathan's palm so she could study it. Even in the face of his obvious reluctance, she wouldn't loosen her insistent grip. "Ah, you have nothing to fear," she reassured him, her voice turning as delicate and sweet as orange blossoms. "Your love line is strong. Unbroken. Your three children will flourish in the light of that love."

Jonathan snatched his hand away, staring at it briefly before he began digging for his wallet. After tossing down several bills, he sprang to his feet and grasped Cassy's elbow, pulling her up and away from the scene.

One of Mother's arms swept out in a dramatic gesture, her gold and silver bracelets jangling like sleigh bells. "Wait, wait. Don't you want to know about—"

"Some other time," Cassy interrupted, tossing an imploring look over her shoulder. She heard Jonathan snarl.

"But, Charlotte, he's your—"

Herbert rose, and in the process of inserting his substantial bulk between them and Mother's ill-timed prophecy, mercifully drowned out her final word. At least Cassy hoped Jonathan hadn't heard her say "destiny." Of all times for Helen to show up. Cassy directed a smile along with her circled thumb and index finger at the wrestler, halting the short, unlikely parade that was lining up to follow them.

Once they were out in the hot, blinding sun, Jonathan gulped a few deep breaths. "Sorry." He seemed to catch the harsh tension in his voice and checked it at once. "All that psychic garbage gives me the creeps. It's as phony as her jewels."

Cassy was one of the few people who knew that Helen's flashy gemstones were genuine—as authentic as her predictions usually were. But Jonathan wouldn't want to hear that, either. "Don't worry about it," she said, giving his arm an encouraging squeeze. "Mother is first and foremost an entertainer. If you keep that in mind, she can be a real stitch."

When he didn't reply, Cassy guessed the humor of the situation still eluded him. "I really do have to be going," she said, and started toward her car. She was beginning to resent the prior commitments that interfered with every chance she had to be with Jonathan. Right after their first unsatisfying phone conversation, she'd driven to Oklahoma and spent almost two weeks working with various members of the medical team who'd be traveling with her to Honduras.

"Would you like to go someplace else for dinner?"

She took it as a good sign that he was still interested enough to ask. But Cassy again detected hesitance, almost as if he expected—or wished—she would turn down the invitation. Which was exactly what she had to do, though not by choice. "You couldn't sway me

Indulge a Little Give a Lot

FREE GIFTS BY MAIL

With proofs-of-purchase plus postage and handling

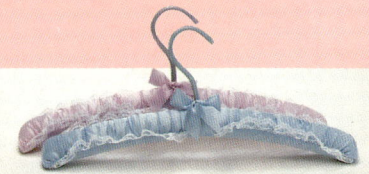

Indulge yourself with these irresistible gifts and at the same time help raise up to $100,000 for **Big Brothers/Big Sisters Programs and Services** in the United States and Canada.

Indulge a Little
Give a Lot

Wonderful, luxurious free gifts can be yours with proofs-of-purchase from specially marked Harlequin or Silhouette books plus postage and handling. And for every specially marked "Indulge A Little" Harlequin or Silhouette book purchased during October, November and December Harlequin/Silhouette will donate 5¢ toward **Big Brothers/Big Sisters Programs and Services** in the United States and Canada for a maximum contribution of $100,000.

Gifts include a beautiful porcelain collector's doll that brings to life the look and feel of the Old South (consumer value $65.00), European-formulated soaps in a handsome, natural willow basket (consumer value, individually packaged, $25.00), a wonderful lace sachet filled with potpourri (consumer value $12.00) and fragrantly scented satin-and-lace hangers (consumer value, package of two, $5.00).

See advertisement on last page for proof-of-purchase and offer certificate.

PRINTED IN U.S.A.   CI-IND

with the best restaurant in Houston tonight. Not when I've got an offer of cherry Jell-O salad and tuna hotdish."

"What's that?"

She laughed at his skeptical tone. "Mostly tuna and noodles, plus some cream of mushroom soup. Down here you call them casseroles, but it's a hotdish to Mrs. Nowicki and me."

"Mrs. Nowicki," he echoed, sounding bewildered and slightly disoriented. "Should I know her?"

"She's a transplanted Minnesotan, like I am. Only she moved down to escape the cold and be closer to her son. She lives four blocks from me, and we have a deal. Every six months she cooks my favorite meal, and I give her a home permanent."

Jonathan sent her an odd look, as if he were trying to picture her winding up someone's hair on tiny pink rods.

Cassy had no false illusions about his original opinion of her. But this meeting was a beginning, and little by little, she would explode every one of his misconceptions.

"Since I can't talk you out of that, what if—" He broke off, glaring at the old Chrysler. "You drive *this*?"

Jonathan sounded like Meredith and practically everyone else she knew. Cassy had never understood why most people were obsessed with cars. The only thing she required from a vehicle was that it get her where she needed to go. A quick scan of the parking area told her which car belonged to Jonathan. The sleek BMW suited him, she supposed, but to Cassy it represented money that could be spent on more essential things. She quickly reprimanded herself. Everyone had a right to spend money on whatever pleased them.

"This is a joke, right?" Jonathan was cringing at a few rusted-out spots on the lower rear quarter panel.

"Do you see me laughing?" Viewing the damage through his critical eyes, Cassy had to admit it was a bit worse than some isolated spots. But a little rust wouldn't keep the car from running effectively. Semi-effectively, she revised. It did have a couple of minor idiosyncrasies. Which reminded her...

Out of the corner of her eye, she saw Jonathan shake his head when she released the hood, then opened the trunk.

"Good grief. Do you own an oil company?" he asked, eyeing several dozen cases of motor oil.

"Personally, I don't own one share of any kind, much less a whole company. I just like to stock up when I catch sales or rebates." She selected a quart, located her pour spout and a rag and went back to the front of the car.

He followed on her heels. "What are you doing?"

What she was doing was so apparent that it was hard to say "I'm going to add a quart of oil" without sounding snide.

"Here, let me do it." Jonathan grabbed the can and viciously punctured the top, spraying a few greasy drops on his immaculate cuff. While he waited for the oil to drain, he stared at her. "Why in God's name are you driving around in this relic? You're a Laurens."

Dismayed by the bite in his voice, Cassy realized that Jonathan was not one of those men impressed by family name and money. She might have been relieved had he been merely indifferent instead of disdainful. "What does being a Laurens have to do with anything?"

"Only someone who's rich could ask a thing like that."

She sighed and disposed of the empty oilcan in a plastic bag she carried for that purpose. Then she slammed down the hood and faced him. "This is a subject I try to avoid, but I can see that we'd better get it out of the way right now.... First," she said, pointing her forefinger at him, "Laurens is my name. You can't expect me to apologize for something I was born with."

"Cassy—"

"No, you brought up the issue. Now you're going to listen. It won't take long." She raised another finger. "Second, I have no connection with the corporation, and that includes income. My grandfather, who founded the company, was a virtual despot about that. You don't work for Laurens—you don't get a dime. It makes everything very simple."

"But surely—"

"I can't deny that I have access to money from another source. However, I don't care much for spending it on myself." Cassy didn't enjoy being goaded into revealing details about her wealth. At some point, Jonathan would have to be told. But until he knew her better, she'd prefer not to mention the size of her trust fund.

She tossed the pour spout and rag into the trunk, slammed it, then hopped into the car, gasping when the steering wheel seared her hand like a branding iron. "In other words, anyone in the market for a society heiress type had better keep on looking, 'cause I ain't it. Stick around and you'll find that out pretty fast."

Cassy cranked the ignition, and the old Chrysler started like a high-performance machine. But Jon noted its noisy reverberation and the clank of a vibrating tail pipe. He'd have to be sure it got a new muffler before the inspection sticker came due next month. *Wait a minute! What's going on here?* Jon was known for his attention to details. The trait, however, had never extended to the maintenance of any woman's car. He was pondering the meaning of that when Cassy took off with a jaunty wave and left him standing motionless in a gritty cloud of dust.

He watched the car lumber away like some Stone Age behemoth, its reddish left haunch standing out noticeably from the rest of its light blue body. He stuffed both hands into his trouser pockets, shaking his head while he listened to her departure. Even with the din of rush hour traffic on North Durham, he could still track her progress for at least a block.

When the distinct sound faded, he ambled toward his car. Like his shoes, it now sported a fine coating of dust. Normally he would head straight to the nearest car wash. But the only place he wanted to drive from here was after the lady who'd just left him. Damnation! He'd never met a woman so hard to categorize as Cassy Laurens. Usually people were fairly easy for him to read, women included. But Cassy wasn't typical by any definition. And that was driving him crazy.

When he'd learned her identity, Jon had collected all the information he could find on Laurens. Except there hadn't been any mention of Cassy or siblings, and not all that much about the company. Laurens, second-generation pioneers in pharmaceuticals and medical technology, was reputedly one of the largest privately held corporations in the country. As such it wasn't subject to the disclosure requirements that applied to publicly owned companies. Guessing its worth was about as reliable as a crapshoot.

Not that Laurens's worth mattered after what she'd told him earlier. The plain truth was that the source of Cassy's money wasn't important. Only that she had a pile of it. So why couldn't he just write her off as he would anyone else in the same situation?

Because she refused to conform to the nice neat stereotype he wanted to pin on her. She hung out with a mixed bag of unique—no, weird—people and frequented places Jon didn't even know existed. Her clothes looked as though they were of good quality, but he doubted they carried designer labels. He'd noticed right away that her plain quartz watch had a cracked crystal. And that car should have been junked a decade ago. From the stash in her trunk, it must guzzle more oil than most Third World countries.

Which led to the most surprising disclosure of all. He didn't know a lot about the Peace Corps, but enough to realize that volunteers didn't lead a cushy life. Cassy had served not one, but two tours in Latin America.

Why would anyone with her background and opportunities choose to endure hardship and deprivation? It didn't make sense.

No, Charlotte Cassidy Laurens was not the typical pampered socialite that he could easily dismiss without a second thought.

And that wasn't the worst of it. He liked her looks. Too much, and in ways he wasn't totally comfortable with. Jon made it a point to never allow the physical side of a relationship to develop before he had a thorough understanding of the woman's personality and, more importantly, her expectations. He was a long way from figuring out Cassy, but he was already perilously close to wanting her.

How could a single braid hanging over her shoulder be sexy? Cassy's was, with those little wisps feathering her forehead, in front of her ears and along the contour of a graceful nape. He didn't like red lipstick, but again and again his eyes had been drawn to her exquisitely formed lips. On her the red looked clear and natural. Just right for kissing. Jon scrambled inside his car, wondering why he'd been standing out in the scorching heat. He started the engine and switched on the air conditioning to let the interior cool for a few minutes before starting home.

By closing his eyes he could reconstruct a picture of Cassy in his mind. At first glance, her eyes had appeared gray. But a closer look revealed the narrow light blue ring that rimmed her inner iris. Whatever the color, they were beautifully animated and expressive, reflecting her mood.

She wasn't afraid to say what was on her mind, either. Her honesty had disarmed him several times during their short meeting. When she'd said "stick around," it was almost as if she were daring him to come after her. She wouldn't have to wait long for that.

"Holy hell," Jon exclaimed. He'd been so rattled by her that he forgot to arrange another meeting. "No problem," he assured himself, shifting the car into Drive. He had her phone number. And the next time he called, it wouldn't be some trumped up excuse.

They hadn't gotten around to discussing why he wanted to see her in the first place. Maybe that was a good thing. It was a pretty flimsy excuse. He really didn't need her signature on a release; it wasn't likely that she would claim the trip later. She had been adamant about not going to Aruba.

Too bad, he thought, edging into the outward-bound flow on Allen Parkway. Because, whether she knew it or not, Cassy was going on that trip with him. Even if he had to keep up the pressure for months, ultimately he'd get her to agree.

It didn't escape Jon's notice that he had done a complete reversal since the auction. No, he told himself. It was more a realignment of priorities. That was another thing he'd learned long ago. Success and flexibility went hand in hand.

CASSY DOUBLE-CHECKED the clock when she saw only five minutes had passed since she'd last looked at it. The Saturday paper was scattered over her oak dining table, but she couldn't work up much enthusiasm for the usual ration of grim tidings. An early riser, she'd planned to be on her way to Galveston by now. Instead, she had an hour to kill before going to an event she had no interest in. No, that wasn't quite accurate. She had a definite interest in one of its participants, which was the reason she was still here.

Last night, only minutes after she returned from Mrs. Nowicki's, Jonathan had phoned to invite her to a street race he was running in this morning. Shocked to hear from him so soon, Cassy had been on the verge of accepting when she cautioned herself against being too eager. She compromised by saying she'd make it if she could rearrange some things.

She had made it sound as though she had appointments in Galveston, but the trip was mainly for fun. She did need to shop for a few gifts and pick up some rugged clothing at the surplus center. That might be loosely construed as business. Mostly she just liked going to the island city that was such a charming combination of tourist kitsch and elegant restorations.

Today was one of the few completely free days she'd have for weeks. As her departure date for Honduras neared, final plans and preparations would swing into high gear. Which made it even more essential to see Jonathan this morning.

Besides, she'd gladly postpone almost anything to see him in a pair of shorts. She'd begun to worry that a wardrobe of three-piece suits had been permanently grafted to what she suspected was a marvelous body. Today she'd know for certain if her suspicions were correct.

Cassy poured another glass of orange juice and giggled at her lustful thoughts. She tried to concentrate on the ScrabbleGram, but gave up after a few attempts. She was too anxious for time to pass. It was new and exciting to feel this fluttery anticipation over seeing a man. Six years with the Peace Corps had provided a wonderful sense of camaraderie and several long-lasting friendships. But romance, while not forbidden outright, was discouraged. Following her return, most of the men she'd dated had been interesting companions, but none had sparked her emotions, her passion. Now she knew why.

She had been waiting for Jonathan Manning. And at last he was hers. Well, almost.

Cassy went into the bedroom and headed straight for the closet. Yesterday she had dressed to create a certain impression. Her demure cotton sweater and skirt were unremarkable. Today, without being too overt, she wanted Jonathan to know she was a woman. Cassy wished her mother had warned her that capturing a reluctant man's attention was such a tricky proposition.

Fortunately the race ended at the intersection of Westheimer and Montrose, only a few blocks from her fourplex. She could get there at the approximate arrival time of the fastest runners and only have to stand in the heat and humidity a few minutes until Jonathan crossed the finish line.

He'd said that, even though it wasn't one of his favorite things to do, he was a fairly good runner. Something about a low fat-to-muscle ratio making his body ideally constructed for running. Envisioning his ideally constructed, sweat-soaked body was doing unmentionable things to hers.

JON GRABBED A TOWEL that someone thrust toward him seconds after he crossed the finish line. He bent at the waist and buried his face in it, fighting for breath. Every year he swore it was the last time he'd run this race. And every year some zealot from the alumni association prevailed on his loyalty to Texas A&M. They always used the same argument: the shame his alma mater would endure if their detestable rivals from the University of Texas won this challenge match. Apparently it was a sound enough reason. Every year the number of masochists increased.

"I've always thought Fun Run is a contradiction in terms."

Jon straightened at the sound of Cassy's voice, a little surprised and a lot relieved to find her there. Last night she hadn't sounded too enthusiastic about changing her plans.

"That pretty well sums up how I feel right now. It was only 5-K, but I wouldn't call it fun."

"You finished fast," she said. "Congratulations."

He could see her tracking the twin paths of moisture snaking down his bare chest, pooling at his waist. "Yeah, fast." He ran the towel roughly over his midsection and wondered if his breathing would ever return to normal. Not a chance, he decided, unless she stopped looking at him like that. The caress of her eyes had suddenly turned him hotter than the August sun.

In contrast, Cassy looked cool and appealing, even more so than she had last night. She had on white walking shorts, which accentuated her long, slender legs. His first impression of her delicacy lingered, but that was due mostly to her fine features and bone structure. In height, she was average or above.

The blue collar of her sailor blouse intensified that shade in her eyes, overshadowing the gray. A twist of red-and-blue ribbon was interwoven into the single braid that hung over her shoulder and brushed against her breast.

Jon cleared his throat and pretended to be absorbed in some runners straining to take a few seconds off their finish time. "You must have been able to call off your date for the beach." A trip to Galveston was synonymous with going to the beach, and last night when she mentioned rearranging things, he had assumed she meant a date. He was encouraged that she'd broken it in favor of seeing him. Conversely, uncharacteristically, the idea of Cassy going out with another man irritated him out of all proportion.

"Stewart Beach or hell. Not a dime's worth of difference." When his startled gaze snapped back to her, she gave him an angelic smile. "Both too hot and crowded, if you ask me."

He laughingly agreed and took a couple of steps back, aware that he probably smelled like a wet sheep and looked worse. "Let's get out of here so I can grab a shower and change. My car's parked one street over." Without touching, he guided her in the right direction.

"Wait a minute," Cassy protested. "I have to pick up *my* car. I put off leaving until later, but I'm still going to Galveston."

Jon felt a muscle in his cheek tense, and he stopped to stare down at her. "In other words, you didn't break the date. Just delayed it." Was that really him sounding so angry and possessive?

"I don't know why you keep bringing up a date," she said patiently. "It's mainly a shopping trip, and I'm going alone."

His expression lightened immediately. "Not anymore, you're not. As of right now, you have a date." Again he started her in the proper direction. "We'll run by my place first, and I'll clean up. We can still make it to Galveston for lunch. And on the way back, we'll stop in Kemah. I promised my partner I'd pick up something for him there."

"This must be why you're so successful," Cassy complained teasingly once she was seated in his car. "Quick decisions followed by forceful action."

Jonathan looked at her, his eyes solemn and unfathomable. "I know how to go after what I want, Cassy. You might keep that in mind."

3

AS THEY SPED AWAY from the Montrose, Cassy was feeling buoyant. She'd been foolish to toy with the idea of playing hard to get, however briefly. It was such a waste of time when she really wanted to be with Jonathan. Wasting time was almost as offensive to her as throwing away money.

Cassy could still hear Meredith's lecture about how she ought to make Jonathan pursue her harder. Her friend was convinced that males, hunters by nature, seldom appreciated easily won victories. They both knew the advice was useless. Cassy had neither the skill nor tolerance for such machinations. Intuitively she knew that Jonathan didn't, either. His insistence on going to Galveston with her had to mean that he wanted to be with her. Things were working out nicely and even faster than she had hoped.

"If you don't care for running, why get out in the hottest month of the year and punish yourself?" She listened to his explanation of alumni coercion while indulging herself in a leisurely once-over of his long, sinewy body. He'd pulled on a T-shirt when they reached the car, but not before Cassy had stored away an indelible image of a tanned, sleekly muscled chest and intriguing patterns of damp, dark hair.

Visually working her way down from a set of suitably broad shoulders, the terrain narrowed over torso and waist. Lower still... Cassy swallowed. Had she been out of the country when men's shorts changed into such brief, blatantly revealing attire?

"I beg your pardon?" she said, caught with a half-guilty smile on her face. He'd asked a question while she had been cataloging his assets. Jonathan braked for a red light before looking at her. One of the first things Cassy had noticed was how his eyes glittered with intelligence. Today they also gleamed with something singularly male—an awareness that Cassy wasn't going to be coy about acknowledging.

"I asked what you do for exercise."

"Uh-oh. Better let me out now if fitness is a prerequisite for this friendship." She made a big production of reaching for her seat belt. "You are looking at a person who lives in mortal terror of being abducted and taken to an upscale health club where I'll be forced to perform unnatural acts on machines."

He laughed, a richly satisfied sound that filled her with pleasure. "Does that mean I'm off the hook, Jonathan?"

"I believe in people doing what they like and enjoy, not what someone else thinks is good for them. Whatever *you* do—or don't—works. Anyone can see that."

Cassy was pleased by the compliment. Good looks weren't that important, she knew, but it didn't hurt that she and Jonathan found each other attractive. What an insipid word for his effect on her. Devastating was more accurate.

During the drive to his high rise near Memorial Park, they traded stories about how her best friend and his business partner had talked them into participating in the bachelor auction against their wishes.

"I was dead set against the idea," Jonathan said, "but I couldn't let Pat down. Now I'm glad I had no choice."

Telling her she was the most gorgeous, ravishing creature in the universe couldn't have charmed her more. She almost said so.

When they arrived at his condo, Jonathan showered and dressed while Cassy gave herself a quick tour of the living area. White walls; black suede dining chairs; glass dining table; chrome vertical blinds; white sofa and lounge chairs; black marble fireplace. A spare arrangement of red anthuriums on the glass table provided the only hint of color or warmth. She peeked into the adjoining kitchen and wrinkled her nose. It was a study in white except for plump red cushions on the breakfast chairs. The overall effect looked like some decorator's concept of how a fast-track bachelor should live.

She gave it high marks as a showcase of minimalist chic. But Cassy didn't like it very much. The place was aloof. It reflected Jonathan's exterior without any traces of the heart of the man. She wanted to look beyond the surface gloss, find some clues to his personality.

The seascape over a slate-topped sideboard in the dining room showed promise. Its soft colors and muted images probably offended the designer's sensibilities. Cassy imagined Jonathan had insisted that it be hung there to offset the starkness of everything else.

Scolding herself for being a snoop didn't stop Cassy from marching into the kitchen and investigating the refrigerator. Her lips curved up at the sight of the cold cuts, cheeses, dips, deli salads, fruit and beer that cluttered the shelves. Unmistakable signs of a single person who probably didn't like to cook, yet didn't particularly enjoy eating out all the time. Cassy understood that. She snitched a few green grapes and popped them into her mouth before wandering back into the living room.

She scooped up a figurine on her way to check out the view from the wall of bronze-tinted windows. Ten stories below she could see the colorful, meticulously sculpted formal gardens of Bayou Bend, an estate that now belonged to the Museum of Fine Arts.

The view slipped out of focus as she imagined Jonathan standing in this spot every morning, eyes heavy with sleep, his voice low and husky like a lover's. The fantasy became more vivid. She was beside him, sampling the distinctive masculinity of him—beard, silky chest hair, smooth skin of his back...

Her fingers rubbed absently over the art object in her hand without looking at it. Cool and sinuous to the touch, it soothed the senses as effectively as tracing worry beads. Only worry beads didn't...

Cassy gaped down at the figure, and her hands suddenly turned moist. Though the obsidian form was abstract, she knew it represented woman. Nothing else could curve so voluptuously, recline so languidly, invite so wantonly. The lady might be glass, but she begged to be stroked. She was flagrantly sensual, and if Jonathan had selected her, Cassy was inclined to heed Meredith's warning. Visualizing herself unleashing Jonathan's volcanic passion made her stomach ripple, her legs tingle.

She replaced the figurine and sank onto the couch, deciding she'd better concentrate on something less distracting. It was all in her mind, anyway. No doubt that statue had been professionally picked to complement the decor, not as an example of Jonathan's taste in erotica. Cassy tipped her head back against the textured cushion, and for the first time she spied a small balcony above one end of the living room. Cleverly angled walls of floor-to-ceiling bookshelves formed a cozy alcove for a single leather Eames chair. It was the one spot she could imagine being comfortable in an otherwise austere environment. She had a feeling Jonathan spent a lot of time there.

Wanting to check out his book collection, Cassy glanced around for the stairs to that level. Before she could spot them, he reappeared, spicy smelling and sharp looking in chinos and a short-sleeved madras shirt.

"Why the puzzled look?"

"That balcony is really nifty. I just can't figure out how to—"

"Secret stairway," he said softly, riveting her with a look that made everything, apart from the two of them, fade into the background. "Next time you're here, I'll show you. It's in my bedroom."

Cassy met his gaze with confidence, but she was relieved that she'd sat down a few moments ago. Even seated, her knees felt totally unreliable. "I'll look forward to it."

His mouth opened; he took a couple of quick, deep breaths. "Oh, Cassy. Why does being with you fill me with dangerous ideas?"

JONATHAN HANDLED the usual crush of beach-bound weekend traffic with an easy competence that Cassy admired. Silly, she told herself, but there was something reassuring about a man who maneuvered and controlled his car with so little effort. She'd never analyzed it before, but in a strictly primitive sense, it made a woman feel secure and protected.

There she went on another flight of fancy! Her encounter with that statue had been only the beginning. Maybe there was something in the air messing up her normally rational way of thinking. She sniffed, then wrinkled her nose. "Oh, yuck, Texas City," Cassy said, pointing at the billowy white clouds spewing out of smokestacks. "I know there are millions of regulations, but I'll never believe anything that smells so nasty isn't toxic."

"Look at it this way. When you get close enough to smell the refineries, the beach isn't much farther." Jonathan pointed in the other direction, away from the trailing stream of emissions.

The lowland had gradually given way to marshes and stretches of shallow water. Houses were perched on blocks or pilings, and most had boats tethered along the network of canals that bounded their backyards.

They were on the twin bridges spanning Galveston Bay when Cassy gave in to impulse. "If you're not set on a place to eat lunch, could we go out on Seawall?" she asked, naming the wide boulevard that paralleled the beach.

Jonathan shrugged and took the exit for a shortcut to the water. "I thought you didn't care about the beach."

"I don't. It's dumb to spend hours in the sun when it's so bad for you. But I love munching hot dogs while I amble along and watch everyone else stretched out like fish in a frying pan."

He shot her an odd look but said nothing. Within minutes they were queued up behind perennially tan regulars and sunburned vacationers with zinc-oxide-smeared noses. Well-developed refugees from Muscle Beach in their tiny Speedo bathing suits cast censuring glances at those with too-ample middles.

"Hot dogs, the great American equalizer," Jon said wryly, ordering two when it was finally their turn.

Cassy thought about asking for an extra, but decided not to push her luck. She guessed she ought to expose Jonathan to her eating habits a little at a time. She could easily put away more food than most men, but Meredith was forever reminding her that it wasn't very feminine to chow down like a field hand. Though Cassy didn't ordinarily subscribe to the theory that you had to sacrifice to appeal to men, maybe she'd make an exception just this once.

They claimed their food and soft drinks, then braved four lanes of traffic to cross to the water side. Winding their way through scores of teenagers draped over folding loungers and plastic rafts, Cassy said, "You know, I've never figured out this phenomenon of coming to the beach and sitting in the back of pickup trucks or on the sidewalk."

"I think the object is to hang out and be seen. Or maybe to couch."

She giggled at the sight he was referring to. "'Heavily bad,' I think is how Meredith would describe it." A pair of young men lolled on a mustard-colored sofa that they had hoisted astride their pickup bed. Ice chest between them, rap music blasting from their portable CD player, they surveyed the sea of humanity below them, especially those clad in teeny bikinis.

"Let's take our picnic out on a jetty," Jonathan suggested, motioning her onto one of the rocky projections that were spaced every few hundred yards. They sat on large flat stones facing each other and placed the food between them.

Cassy bit into her hot dog, aware that Jonathan was sipping his cola and watching her. She chewed slowly, marveling at how she could feel so right being with him and at the same time buzzing with nervous energy. Driven to relieve the inexplicable tension, she said, "It's a lot cooler out here on the jetty."

"Mmm," he murmured, transferring his gaze to the grayish water. "When I was about six, my dad started bringing me down here almost every weekend. We'd fish, have a picnic lunch, walk on the beach sometimes. After they opened up more attractions for tourists, we'd occasionally take in one of those. But mostly we fished and talked, just the two of us. I never get tired of looking at the ocean."

She was grateful he'd shared that small slice of his past. It was the sort of thing couples did at the beginning of a relationship. "I know what you mean. I grew up on one of Minnesota's ten thousand plus lakes."

His eyes cut back to her. "In a mansion, I suppose."

Cassy's good spirits of a moment ago waned. "There are plenty of homes on Minnetonka that can be called mansions. Ours isn't one of them." Appetite gone, she tossed her crumpled napkin and remaining food into a paper bag. "No limo and chauffeur, either."

"I didn't mean that as a condemnation," he said, reacting quickly to the defiance she hadn't bothered to mask. "I'm curious, I guess. Not about your house, though. Just you."

"Oh," she whispered, elation welling up inside her. He'd already modified his initial impression of her as spoiled rich girl enough to admit he didn't know her at all. "Ask me anything. You won't find any locked doors. I'm a simple woman, Jonathan."

He leaned forward slightly and planted both palms flat on the stone between them. "You, Cassy Laurens, are many things. I don't think 'simple' is one of them."

His eyes were the deep green of moss on river rocks as they dwelled first on her eyes, her nose, her mouth, then down to the modest V neckline of her sailor blouse and back up. Through parted lips, her breathing turned quick and shallow, matching his. Cassy had to fight closing her eyes in preparation for his kiss. At that moment she wanted it more desperately than air.

He wanted it, too. She could see that clearly. But he didn't move closer, merely continued to regard her intensely while he waged some internal battle. When it became obvious there would be no kiss, several explanations occurred to Cassy. One possibility was so disturbing she had to ask.

Her heart was pounding out a drumbeat of dread. "Are you involved with someone else, Jonathan?"

"No," he answered readily, and she believed him. "I haven't been for a long time."

Relief was so welcome, she decided to forget all the other reasons he wouldn't give in to the passionate spark that had bound them for a few seconds. "How about an ice-cream cone for dessert?"

"Cassy—"

"My treat," she said, tugging him to his feet. There would be plenty of time later to analyze Jonathan's hesitation in a situation where most men would have pressed their advantage.

He drove to the Strand, a street lined with restored buildings, funky shops and eateries. Cassy made a beeline for the turn-of-the-century ice-cream parlor. Since it was her treat, she insisted that Jonathan choose first. His single dip of cookies-and-cream might have restrained a less dedicated ice cream fancier. But not her. She ordered one scoop each of the three most colorful flavors in the case. Ignoring his raised brow, she started for the door. "Let's window-shop while we eat."

Back on the Strand, Cassy was immediately drawn to a display of Guatemalan worry dolls. As she admired the dolls and the surrounding draping of vintage clothing, she caught a glimpse of herself and Jonathan in the glass. Her eyes widened; the flame of desire flickered to life deep inside her. His gaze was locked on her mouth while her tongue swirled with hungry abandon around and over the ice cream. For a breathless moment she couldn't look away, couldn't even think why she should.

At last he touched her elbow, his hand hot and damp, and they moved in tandem away from the telltale reflection. Cassy was melting in Jonathan's heat quicker than ice cream in the summer sun.

"Where to next?" he asked, his voice sounding controlled in spite of the faint hoarseness.

"Where else? Colonel Bubbie's." Much as she'd like, this busy Galveston street was the last place to explore the sensual awareness that seemed to be overtaking them like a runaway train.

"You came all the way down here to shop at that kind of store? Why?"

"I hate shopping in general. So I order practically everything from catalogs. But Bubbie's is special. I love poking around in there."

"I might have guessed," Jonathan grumbled good-naturedly.

The Strand Surplus Center may have started out as a typical army surplus outlet, but it had far eclipsed the original concept. Cassy had been there many times and always left with the feeling that she'd missed some hidden treasures.

Today the first thing that caught her eye was the sign, We Make Dog Tags. Maybe she'd look into getting those for her teams of volunteers as a souvenir of their tour of duty.

Inside the main room it was hot, crowded and musty smelling, with a hodgepodge of clothing and military artifacts stacked or hanging from every available inch of space. Cassy headed toward a display of army pants.

She riffled through the assortment of olive pants that had two huge patch pockets on the rear and buttons at both sides of the waist. "Would you mind waiting while I try these on?" she asked, skipping down a couple of steps to the fitting rooms without waiting for an answer.

Not only were the pants the right size, they were comfortable and durable, just what she'd need for Honduras. She decided to buy six pairs. Cassy knew from experience that doing laundry by hand in primitive settings was a pain. She found Jonathan beneath a brown-and-orange parachute that was suspended from the ceiling like a canopy. He was studying a dilapidated wooden sleigh crammed with snowshoes, canteens and other survival gear.

He eyed her armload of fatigues. "What are you planning to do with all those? Lead a commando raid?"

"Not exactly." She was eager to tell Jonathan about the project that had consumed her for months. Hopefully, learning of her dedication to something worthwhile would do away with his remaining reservations. It was essential that he take her seriously. This just wasn't the time or place to get into a detailed explanation. "I need this kind of clothing for where I'm going in a couple of months. I'll be roughing it."

She expected a startled look followed by the obvious question. But after a long silence, he said, "I hope you aren't planning to be gone long."

She could interpret his simple statement several ways, the most promising one being that Jonathan didn't want her to be away because he wanted to see her on a regular basis. Cassy wanted that, too, but she had to face facts. For more than a year, her work had demanded almost every waking moment. Not many men would put up with that. "Uh, it's not definite yet how long I'll have to stay."

He didn't reply, although his expression hinted that he found her vague answer unsatisfactory.

Looking around for a diversion, she spotted a stack of thirteen-button flap Navy blues. "Oh, wonderful!" She put aside her stack of folded pants and dug into the pile of dark blue wool. "Did you know these are called crackerjacks?"

"Can't say I did." His voice was edged with impatience.

"This will only take a second. I promise." Cassy fitted a pair to Jonathan's waist. "He's about your height but has a few pounds on you. A few inches around the middle, too."

"Who?" he asked gruffly.

"My father. He collects nautical memorabilia. I've already found him an antique brass ship's telegraph for his birthday. But these will be his fun gift."

She kept the pants plastered against Jonathan with one hand. "I'll bet you also don't know what the thirteen buttons stand for."

"No." His admission sounded painful.

"Everything on a naval uniform has significance. These buttons, for instance, represent the first thirteen states." Her fingers grasped the top one and counted down. "Delaware, Pennsylvania, New Jersey. All of them ratified the constitution in 1787. Then the next year Georgia, Connecticut, Massachusetts, Maryland, South Carolina—"

"Cassy," Jonathan said through gritted teeth. "Would you head north? Real quick."

"Oh, sorry." She stepped back, fingers gripping the waist of the pants. "American history has always fascinated me."

"That's fine. I just don't make a very good map."

"Sorry," she said again, realizing she had embarrassed him. She'd had him pinned against a shelf, her hands roaming over a very sensitive portion of his anatomy. And his body had reacted predictably, even though she honestly hadn't meant to arouse him. "Let me pay for these, and we'll get out of here."

Back on the street, they walked in silence. When they reached the car, Jonathan unlocked the trunk and neatly arranged her parcels alongside a gym bag and a pair of basketballs.

"Cassy, about what happened back there..." He clasped his hands behind him and stared at the unusual arch bridging the Strand. "It's not that I don't like you touching me, but—" His hands slipped into his pockets. He kicked at a small pebble with one foot. At last he looked at her, his face taut with frustration. "It felt good, okay? Too damned good for my peace of mind."

"If it's any consolation, I did it without thinking. I pride myself on being straightforward, but I don't make a practice of feeling up men in public places." She gave him her most guileless smile. "I don't, however, make promises about what I might do in private. If that scares you, Jonathan, I guess you'd better keep your distance."

"Stop laughing at me, you little minx. You know damn well I'm not going to do that. But I have the feeling you already know I'm going to be seeing a lot of you. So why don't you call me Jon, like my friends do."

Cassy tested the name on her tongue, tapping down the urge to tell him they were going to be much more than friends. Or perhaps, if she was lucky, he was already thinking along those lines.

They left the car parked where it was and strolled down the wharf to tour the tall ship *Elissa*, a restored 1877 square-rigger. And afterward, when Jon held her hand during the entire open-air "train" excursion around the island, Cassy couldn't remember any day in her life that had been more magical. It was late afternoon when he reminded her of their detour through Kemah, adding that they'd eat dinner there after he'd taken care of the favor to his partner.

By the time they got to the little town located on a channel that connected Clear Lake with Galveston Bay, the clouds had darkened. A brisk wind whipped in off the bay and whitecaps dotted the water. "Looks like we're in for a storm," Cassy commented, apprehensively scanning the sky.

"Uh-huh. But it won't amount to much."

"How can you tell?" She pointed at the steady procession of boats streaming in under power. "All those people must be taking it seriously."

"I have a feel for weather. It interests me. Always has. It's a hobby of mine." Jon opened his door. "I have to check a couple of things on Pat's boat. Come with me. It won't take long, then we can have dinner."

There were hundreds of slips, most of them full. As they made their way to Pat's boat, Cassy glanced at the roiling clouds overhead. She wasn't overly fond of storms, especially of being on water during them. Not to worry, she told herself, hopping nimbly on board. It wasn't raining yet, and Jon had said it wouldn't take long to check the boat. They might even make it back to Houston before the storm hit.

When the first fat drops splatted onto the deck, Cassy hoped Jon's forecasting skills were better than hers. Forget about making it to Houston; they'd do well to get inside. He fished a key out of his pocket and unlocked the companionway door, leading her down the steps just ahead of the downpour. He'd grabbed a flashlight from the cockpit locker and used that to guide their way.

Cassy remained on the bottom step, watching his dark shadow move silently into the cabin. Through the small forward ports she could see dim flashes of lightning heralding the storm's arrival. She locked her knees and braced herself against the bulkhead. Maybe it would pass over quickly.

Jonathan located a battery-powered lantern and came back toward her, its faint glow casting his features in sharp relief. Seeing her rigid stance, he asked, "You okay, Cassy?"

"Fine," she forced herself to say. "Storms make me a little... jumpy, that's all."

"Don't worry about this one," Jon said with quiet reassurance. "It's a lot of thunder and lightning and probably a hard, fast rain. We're perfectly safe here." He stood aside and motioned her forward. "Why don't you look around while I check things out."

Telling herself that Jon knew what he was talking about, Cassy nodded and stepped past him. To keep her mind occupied, she followed his suggestion and inspected the boat's interior. That took all of thirty seconds. When she turned back around, he handed her a small glass half-full of something dark and potent looking.

"What's this?"

"Pat's expensive French cognac. He warned me that he knows exactly how much was left in the bottle the last time he was here." Jon lifted his own glass in a toast. "Drink up. I'll tell him we needed it for medicinal purposes."

Cassy inhaled the heady fumes and took a liberal swallow. It ran through her like a river of fire, all the way to her toes. She knew the immediate relaxation was psychological, but she never argued with success. Instead, she took another sip.

Jon left his drink on the dinette table and took a small sports bag out of the hanging locker. He opened various storage compartments, removing what appeared to be files and stowing them in the bag. Cassy followed him to the forward stateroom, a curious term since it barely had space for two people.

Two people could also sleep there. Not together, though, she thought, measuring the V-berths. Unless they slept very, very close. The way she and Jonathan would.

She sank onto one of the berths and watched him bend to search for something in the forepeak. That position made his slacks hug his backside even more interestingly than they had only seconds ago.

It wouldn't take much to touch him there, guide him onto the opposite berth, stretch him out and...

She'd seen him nearly naked at the race, and this afternoon her fingers had inadvertently skimmed over what his running shorts had concealed. It wasn't hard to merge the visual and tactile sensations into a stirring package of desirable masculinity.

Cassy shook her head and pulled in oxygen rapidly. It was the brandy kicking in, making her fantasize about taking wild, impetuous advantage of Jonathan's body. She had to get control of these fiendish delusions. It was too early in the relationship to even dream about doing anything so forward. If only they had known each other months, or even weeks, she could undo his buttons, her mouth teasing each newly revealed bit of flesh as she eased off his shirt.

Cassy could feel the warmth on her face, her neck, all over. She let out a little moan.

"Cassy?"

"Don't mind me. It's just the barometric pressure playing tricks with my mind. Go on about your business."

He scratched around awhile longer before zipping up the bag and putting it in the main cabin. He came back with his drink and dropped onto the berth across from her. "Mission accomplished," he said, planting one foot on the mattress and extending his other leg. "This boat is Pat's pride and joy. Right now he's stuck in Colorado and is suffering separation anxiety because he can't get down here on weekends."

Cassy tried to smile, but her mouth and lips felt impossibly dry. How could something as simple as Jon's casual pose cause her insides to go all quivery and fluid? Perhaps another small nip of cognac would relieve that. Yes, that definitely helped. "I noticed the name is *Siren*."

"Yeah, and she lures old Pat just like her namesakes."

She watched his thumb rub back and forth over his snifter and wondered what it would take to lure him. "I guess every man deserves one vice."

"He gives her time and attention and money. All the things a man should give his woman."

Cassy swallowed, but it was an effort. His voice was a soft seduction, and her resistance was low. She had never known that desire could be quite this tangible, so potent it could make her weak. "Maybe Pat needs to find a woman to lavish his attention on."

"He has a wife. She bought *Siren* for him and sails with him most of the time. Offhand, I'd say he lavishes the appropriate amount of attention on her. I've never heard Christie complain."

"Women in love seldom complain."

"I guess that's the secret."

It was the quiet, almost reverent way he said it more than the words. Cassy's heart leaped with joy at the underlying message. It told her one thing for sure. He might take a slow and careful approach to it, but Jonathan Manning had a healthy respect for love.

Her main interest was that he think about it now, with her. She gazed deeply into his eyes, willing him to confirm her hope. What she saw made her hands tremble, and she had to use both to steady her glass.

Out in the open he'd been able to ignore or at least suppress the sensual pull. Within these close confines, he was no more immune to it than Cassy. Love might not be on his mind yet, but she was. Within his eyes she saw awareness and wariness, desire and indecision.

"Jon?"

"I want to kiss you."

"That seems to be giving you grief."

"What's giving me grief is that kissing you isn't the only thing I want to do. It can't be happening this fast."

"Sometimes there's no stopping it."

"I can. At least I've always thought I could." He massaged the back of his neck. "What I'm trying to tell you is that I'm ultracautious and deliberate where women are concerned. I need to know a woman a long time before I . . . before we—"

"Make love?"

"Hell, Cassy. Do you always have to be so blunt?" He jumped to his feet.

"Sorry. It's a compulsive habit."

"Forget it. The point is, do you understand?"

"That you're not interested in going to bed with me because we've just met? Yes, I understand." Her gaze unwavering, she moistened her lips. "What do you intend to do about it?"

He drained the brandy glass and shuddered. "I don't seem to be thinking very clearly. Suppose you tell me."

Cassy set her snifter aside and rose. "Why don't we just try the kiss and not worry about what might develop later?"

4

THE TWO SHORT STEPS it took to reach Jonathan felt like the most important ones of Cassy's life. And she'd been waiting a lifetime to take them. He may have shifted the responsibility to her for what came next, but before she even touched him, the message in his eyes was clear. He was through fighting the irresistible link, at least for now.

The second her fingers curved over his shoulders, one of his hands slipped around her waist, the other tipped her chin up, and his mouth came down on hers. Satisfaction flowed over Cassy with that first gentle pressure. She edged closer to him, subtly encouraging.

His lips rubbed back and forth over hers as if he wanted to immerse himself gradually in the shape and feel and taste of her before probing more intimately. He leisurely savored each corner, then followed the upper curve again and again until its fuller mate captured his attention. But for all his control, flesh meeting tender flesh was like spark to tinder. Caught in the resulting blaze, Cassy opened her mouth beneath his, and the quest became bolder, mutual.

Overhead, thunder rumbled in ominous counterpoint to their soft sighs as their tongues touched tentatively before tangling in sensual abandon. She'd imagined his kiss would be like this, yearned for it, knew it would be wonderful. But in her fantasies she hadn't been engulfed by heat and a raw hunger so demanding it made her tremble. She clutched at Jon's back and felt his muscles constrict, then relax beneath her restless fingers.

A sudden, powerful gust of wind slammed into the boat, hurling Cassy against Jonathan's chest and forcing him to step back in order to steady her. As *Siren* strained at her mooring ropes, stormy green eyes clashed with gray. "Cassy?"

"Oh, Jona—"

He swallowed the rest of his name with a kiss, this one deeper, more insistent and provocative. Her eyes drifted shut, not to screen out the violent streaks of lightning but to empty her senses of everything except the man claiming her mouth with such wayward thoroughness.

Jon dragged his lips away only to find an exquisitely responsive spot on the back of her neck. His tongue drew a moist circular pattern, and Cassy whimpered in reaction to the sweet sensations bursting inside her. When he sucked lightly but repeatedly, drawing her sensitive skin inside, she could only cling and cry out from the sharp corresponding pull she felt at her breasts. He hadn't even touched her there; still her body responded as if she'd been caressed . . . and by someone who knew exactly how to do it.

Rain pounded the roof of the cabin. Wind and sea swells combined to lift the boat in gentle undulations that thrust Cassy against Jon, evoking the rhythm of lovemaking.

"Cassy," he whispered roughly, "I want more of you." His hardness nestled against the softness of her stomach. She stood on tiptoe, straining toward the evidence of his desire. A harsh, guttural sound ripped from him, and he backed away to put a safe amount of distance between them. "See why I was worried? See what happened with only a kiss?"

Cassy clasped her fingers together, torn between what both their bodies were aching for and what she knew had to be done. She had thought she understood and accepted her feelings for Jon, but this went far beyond the realm of anything she'd expected. "You were right," she said regretfully, touching his cheek, loving the feel of his evening-rough beard. "We need more time together before I . . . before we—"

"Make love?"

She smiled faintly as he repeated her earlier bluntness. "It's not a crime to be strongly attracted to someone, Jon," she reasoned in their defense.

"Of course it isn't. It's natural. Desirable." He faltered on the last word, then went on determinedly. "But we'll both be able to handle it better further along in our relationship. After we've had the chance to learn more about each other."

Cassy felt a renewed surge of pleasure. He wasn't speaking in generalities now. He'd said "our" relationship and after "we've" learned more about each other. She could be content with that for now. Turning, she cast a saucy look over her shoulder. "Meanwhile, if you're expecting to find out anything else tonight, you're going to have to feed me first."

CASSY SWIPED AT THE TEARS streaming down her cheeks and sniffed loudly. Miserable as she was, there was no alternative except to suffer. In four hours at least twelve people would show up at her door expecting homemade spaghetti sauce.

She picked up a chef's knife and attacked the first of the remaining half dozen onions. She'd already diced six of the grapefruit-size troublemakers and tossed them into a large copper sauté pan with a mound of chopped green peppers. Along with the pungent vegetables, freshly pressed garlic sizzled in extra virgin olive oil. Scrumptious smells already filled her old-fashioned kitchen. Soon the whole building would guess what was on tonight's menu.

Cassy didn't cook for company often, but when she did, everything was made from scratch. Including the tomato sauce and paste she'd stayed up preparing until one o'clock that morning. Like a trooper, Jon had helped her wash and mash a bushel of fresh tomatoes after they'd returned from Kemah. But when she told him the next step involved stirring the mixture for forty-five minutes, he'd tactfully excused himself—after a long, gratifying kiss.

A smile chased her tears as she finished chopping the last onion and transferred it to the pan. Cassy had chided him about not contributing his part to the meal when earlier he'd accepted an invitation to share it. Looking decidedly *un*guilty, he'd offered to supply the wine. When she told him to bring enough for a dozen or more, he had hesitated for only a moment.

She'd been surprising Jonathan since paying a record price for him at the bachelor auction. He had a lot more to learn, but after last night, she knew they were both looking forward to the discovery process. Her only reservation was that long-standing obligations soon would claim the majority of her time.

Time, Cassy reflected, was becoming her worst enemy where Jon was concerned. She hoped he could understand that her dedication to the Honduras project was the only thing significant enough to keep her away from him. An inspection of her calendar this morning had confirmed that his patience was going to be tested right away.

The next day she had to fly to Minneapolis for the scheduled semiannual meeting with the Cassidy foundation directors. After that she planned a side trip to South Dakota. Through her growing network of volunteers, she'd heard about a pharmacist who might be persuaded to join one of the Honduras-bound teams. Since they were short of professionals with that background, she felt obliged to check out the lead. Past experience proved that face-to-face meetings produced a much higher success rate than phone requests.

No sooner would she get back from up north than she'd have to take off for central Texas. An old friend she hadn't seen in years was playing hermit on a hill country spread, and Cassy intended to smoke him out. He topped the list of people whose considerable skills she needed.

So when did that leave room for Jonathan? A week from tomorrow night, if he was free then.

Before she'd found Jon on that fateful night, life had seemed so simple. Well, perhaps not simple, but with clear-cut goals and a plan for attaining them. Now she was torn by conflicting priorities and warring emotions.

Cassy's greatest fear was that someday she'd be forced to choose between the two most important things in her life.

JON SANK A FADEAWAY JUMP SHOT and paused to run a soaked wristband over his dripping face before loping back down court. The other five players were fifteen- and sixteen-year-old boys. They were running him ragged. What kind of idiots charged up and down an outdoor basketball court when the thermometer read nearly a hundred degrees and the humidity was only a few points lower? Nobody but teenagers. Or thirty-four-year-old men driven into action when their thoughts turned too hot to handle in solitary.

Sunday was Jon's day to be alone. He worked long and hard during the week, and Saturdays were usually reserved for taking care of errands or spending time with friends. But Sundays were his to sleep in, read the paper, watch sports, not shave and have food delivered. In short, to be an unrepentant slob. He needed the time to recharge.

Today, however, he'd awakened early, too distracted and jittery to focus on any of his normal activities. He'd finally given up and turned to physical exertion as a means to burn off the excess energy. Jon saw himself as more self-disciplined than most people he knew. He was able to screen out insignificant details and concentrate on what was important. If that was the case, Cassy must now be the only thing that was important. He couldn't think of anything except her and that they'd be together in just a few hours.

Jon had to chase a pass when the ball whizzed by him. Cassy had ruined his concentration again.

He couldn't comprehend precisely what was going on between them or why it was hitting him so hard and fast. His past experiences with women hadn't prepared him for the sudden, intense rush of feelings he'd developed for Cassy. It was especially unsettling since he'd been so positive that he wouldn't like a single thing about her.

But he'd immediately found her disarming, unpretentious, appealing. And to his complete surprise, sexy.

That first taste of her mouth had nearly been his undoing, and for a few frantic minutes, he hadn't cared. Never before had spontaneous passion taken him so far, so quickly. Between them, they'd somehow managed to restore a hormonal equilibrium that lasted through a lengthy dinner and the rest of the evening. When he'd managed to leave her with only a single kiss, he almost had himself convinced that the madness wouldn't possess him again. But today, not even two hours of full-tilt basketball subdued the hot, throbbing urgency that had invaded his dreams and pursued him into wakefulness.

By the time Jon pulled up in front of Cassy's fourplex shortly after six that evening, he'd given himself a series of stern lectures on the advantages of control. He wasn't some horny teenager out to score. He was a mature man, one who recognized the value of a slow getting-acquainted period that, if mutually satisfying, would lead to the added reward of physical intimacy. Intellectually, Jon believed what he'd been telling himself, and he had operated on that premise all his life. Unfortunately, for the past few days his body had refused to cooperate.

He pocketed his keys and started up the walk, once again struck by the modest two-story brick structure. The building was well maintained, its grounds colorfully landscaped, but it was far from lavish. Chalk up yet another eye-opener from the unpredictable Ms Laurens.

Last night he'd made a couple of indirect references to her choice of homes, and Cassy had finally admitted to owning the four-unit building. One of her few "possessions," as she described it, before telling him that she lived on the rental income from the other three apartments. Any way he figured it, that didn't add up to megabucks every month.

What did she do with the money she'd mentioned having access to, money from the unexplained other source? Nothing in Cassy's appearance, demeanor or surroundings typified—or even hinted at—the wealth he'd expected her to flaunt. Jon was fast coming to the conclusion that his time-honored rule book had flown out the window when Cassy Laurens entered his life.

To be honest, he would rather have the lady to himself tonight. But the spaghetti feed had been planned weeks ago and, in her own words, she couldn't abide people who didn't honor commitments. Jon could hardly complain since it was a principle he, too, respected. So he'd have to settle for sharing her with a group of friends. Sooner or later they'd all have to go home. He would stay. At least long enough to ask . . .

Cassy greeted him at the door, looking flushed, expectant and so damned appetizing that he forgot about food and the shopping bag of wine bottles in his hand. She was wearing a strapless dress, three wide bands in jade green, deep rose and lilac made of some light and crinkly fabric. Every centimeter of exposed skin reminded him of a ripe peach, succulent and begging to be ravished.

The Reluctant Bachelor

All his good intentions flew out the window along with the rule book.

How could a woman, Cassy asked herself as she clutched Jonathan's hand, come so close to thirty before experiencing this sizzling, bone-melting attraction to a man? He had on gray dress slacks and a light blue pinstripe oxford cloth shirt, but she was thinking back to yesterday, when he'd worn much less, and ahead to...

"Introduce us, dearest, before the hardwood ignites," Meredith scolded, tapping one three-inch sandal heel against the oak floor.

She looked spectacular in emerald silk, and Cassy prepared to watch Jon go goggle-eyed, which men invariably did when they first saw the tall, fabulous redhead. He didn't even glance at her. "Meredith Winslow, Jonathan Manning."

"Jonathan," Meri purred in her most bewitching voice. "He really is magnificent up close," she added in a brash stage whisper.

"Uh-huh. Magnificent," Cassy agreed. Jon's eyes never strayed from Cassy. They took in the pulse hammering in her neck, then dropped lower to the band holding up the bodice of her dress. Her free hand involuntarily shielded herself from the heat of his gaze.

"Excuse me," Meri said dryly, touching Cassy's shoulder. "It isn't often that I'm extraneous. I'll just go eat tofu and kelp or something."

"Help yourself," Cassy said before her friend's words sank in. Meredith detested health food. Cassy laughed, ending the erotic interlude. Still holding Jon's hand, she urged, "Come on in. You need to meet everyone else."

They unpacked his wine before joining the animated, garrulous crowd. Cassy felt Jon's arm tense as they approached Mother Divine, but he was safe from her psychic readings. Before he arrived, Cassy had a little talk with Helen and told her to put a lid on the predictions.

Cassy stuck close by Jon, making sure that he met everyone and staying to chat briefly with several guests as they circulated. Eventually she had to abandon him to put the finishing touches on the meal.

Jon watched Cassy work her way toward the kitchen, pausing every few feet to speak to someone. No matter who she talked to, they ended up looking happier than before. She had that effect on everyone. Him most of all.

He'd been skeptical about coming to this little get-together. Where once he'd had visions of society snobs surrounding Cassy, all day long a collection of Boise Bonebreakers and Mother Divines had haunted him. But each person he'd talked to seemed interesting and basically normal.

Most of the guests shared a common thread of dedication to something beyond their own personal concerns. He knew that Meredith, like his partner, Pat, was involved with the Hunger Coalition. Jon wondered what cause Cassy claimed. Astounded, he realized that he didn't even know if she had a job, or if not, what she did all day. They had to do some serious talking. Tonight.

Meeting her friends, seeing her interact with them, gave him another insight into the woman who had so far contradicted every bias he'd held against her in advance. She was still rich—that much hadn't changed.

But when he was with her, Jon could almost forget that bothersome detail.

"Our hostess is motioning to you," Rollo, a short, moundlike literature professor said, interrupting Jon's contemplation. "I think it's time to eat."

Meals at Cassy's were informal affairs. Tonight she heaped plates with spaghetti and sauce in the kitchen and passed a huge bowl of salad after everyone was seated. Eight people gathered at her round oak pedestal table; the remaining four found places at a temporary setup in the living room. She'd insisted on serving Jonathan first since he was a newcomer to the group. But by the time Cassy carried in two baskets of garlic bread, he was flanked by Meredith and Rollo, and there were no more seats in the dining room.

She gave him a small shrug of apology along with a tacit promise that their time would come later. He confirmed it with a barely discernible nod of his head. A tiny wave crested in her stomach, replacing hunger pangs. She wished her guests would eat and run.

"Umm, divine, Cass. Your homemade bread is better than my grandmother's. Better than anyone's," Meredith complimented.

Several of the others made affirming sounds, agreeing as politely as they could with full mouths. Cassy smiled when she caught Jonathan's brows lifting in disbelief. It was obvious that he'd never pictured her as a homebody who baked. She watched him bite into a chunk, chew, then lick the butter from his lips. Her heartbeat kicked even more erratically when he winked his approval and slowly sank his teeth into the bread for another taste.

That mistress of ceremonies at the auction had been right. His eyes *were* full of naughty promises.

It wasn't like her to get so flustered, Cassy told herself as she grabbed her plate and fled to the adjoining room. But if Jon held fast to his conviction about not rushing into anything physical, she'd be a basket case. She already was.

When everyone was finished, Cassy stacked plates and individual salad bowls and started for the kitchen. Just before entering the dining room, she caught the question, "Has Cassy enlisted you as one of her Honduras-bound volunteers?" The query came from a local poet in residence, and there could be no doubt to whom it was directed.

Cassy leaned against the doorway, pinned by Jonathan's inscrutable stare. For the life of her, she couldn't read a thing in his cool, unwavering regard.

"As a matter of fact," she began briskly, "Jon and I haven't had a chance to talk much about that." *As a matter of fact*, she mocked silently, *we haven't talked about it at all*. And from the look of him, he considered it a rather significant omission on her part.

"That's right," he said evenly. "Cassy and I have a lot of catching up to do. I'm afraid we skipped a few of the important preliminaries."

She was spared a response to his mild taunt by Rollo's triumphant return from the kitchen.

"Rollo, surely you're not going to eat another plateful of spaghetti," Meredith reprimanded, looking at the rest of the group for support. "Everybody's entitled to an indiscretion now and then. But second helpings of pasta are a no-no." As soon as he sat down, she rapped his knuckles twice for emphasis.

The Reluctant Bachelor

The little man tucked a napkin back into his waistband and lifted his fork with a flourish. "Meri, there are those who view their bodies as temples," he lectured, sounding very much the professor. Then, beaming angelically, he surveyed his audience. "I, on the other hand, have always thought of mine as a rotunda."

Everyone cracked up, including Jonathan. Cassy let out a sigh, relieved to be freed from that penetrating glare, and made her escape to the kitchen.

Several of the others carried in dishes and loaded the dishwasher while Cassy put coffee on to perk and sliced the *cassata perugina* that would be their dessert.

"My God, Charlotte," Helen protested as she swiped her pinky over a dab of frosting. "Is there anything in that recipe that isn't fattening?"

"Hmm, let's see. Pound cake, heavy cream, butter, nuts, ricotta cheese and about a pound of chocolate. I guess not unless we call golden raisins and Grand Marnier low-cal."

"Sinful," the full-figured Helen denounced. "Be sure to give me a big piece. I'm feeling especially imprudent tonight."

Cassy handed her a serving tray filled with dessert plates. "Do me a favor and take these in while I get the cups and saucers."

She was straining to reach the top shelf when a pair of large hands spanned her waist from behind. "So help me, Cassy, when we get rid of these people, I'm sitting you down for a heart-to-heart."

She turned slowly in his grasp. He looked so totally distressed—unnecessarily, in her opinion—that she resorted to teasing. "Are you sitting me in your lap for our heart-to-heart?"

"Hell, no! I'm parking myself clear across the room so there's no way I'll be tempted to touch you."

"But it feels so good when you do, and I know you like it, too."

"Dammit, Cassy. This is serious." He followed her to the refrigerator. "It's time I started finding out about the real C. C. Laurens."

She removed the cream pitcher, handing it to him along with the sugar bowl. "I told you yesterday. I'm not harboring any deep, dark secrets. You can ask me anything."

"You can count on it."

After what seemed like hours, Jon wandered aimlessly around Cassy's living room while she bid farewell to the last of her guests. He halted in front of a black-lacquered breakfront and studied the arrangement of eclectic objects on glass shelves. He browsed through her book and record collections. Her taste in reading and music also defied categorizing.

Eyes closed, he let his head drop forward, chin resting on his chest. The more he learned of Cassy, the more confused he became. It was an unfamiliar predicament for Jon and one he needed to get a handle on.

"Jonathan, are you all right?" Cassy asked softly, switching off the ceiling light in her small entry hall before joining him.

He straightened and walked to the pillow-back swivel chair in a corner. "I'll be fine as soon as I get some answers."

Remembering his earlier admonition that she was to be across the room from him, Cassy chose the camel-back sofa. She kicked off her sandals and stretched out to relax. "Ask away."

The Reluctant Bachelor

He hesitated for a second before collapsing in the chair. "Suppose we start with your 'Honduras-bound volunteers.'"

Cassy had made this presentation so often in the past year that she could recite it in her sleep. "When I served in Latin America, wherever I looked I saw malnutrition, disease, lack of medical care." She took a deep breath to combat the now-familiar tightness in her chest. "You always hear about these tragic conditions in Africa, but believe me, it's every bit as shocking right here in our own backyard. I lived with it every day, and it did something to me."

Jonathan sat forward, hands clenched, eyes unreadable.

"After my two tours, I taught Spanish to Peace Corps recruits, but I just couldn't get away from those images. By the time I came back to the States, I knew I wouldn't be satisfied unless I tried to do something about conditions down there."

She fingered the tuft of hair at the end of her braid, a habit that surfaced only when she contemplated serious matters. "Do you recall when I told you Gran'pa Laurens's philosophy of no work, no benefit?"

He nodded but didn't say anything, so she went on. "The other side of that coin was my Grandfather Cassidy. Beer was his game, and he made a fortune from it." She named a popular brand that got Jonathan's attention. "He left my two brothers, my sister and me all of it, in trust funds that we could each take control of when we turned twenty-five."

"So you *are* wealthy."

"I have access to a lot of money," she said, careful not to even hint at the specific number of millions she had at her disposal. "But strange as it seems, I agree with my paternal grandfather, even if he was an old tyrant. I'm not comfortable living in luxury on money that I didn't earn."

Jon leaped to his feet and stalked over to tinker with her stereo. "But still, you—"

That sounded like the lead-in to an accusation, and Cassy felt the heat of anger suffuse her skin. "An accident of birth made me rich," she snapped. "Look around you!" She gestured at her clothes, the setting. "I'm not really cut out for it."

"Cassy, honey—"

She'd have liked to savor the endearment, but anxious to get this behind her, she interrupted him again. "Anyway, after thinking about it for a long time, I decided that what I really wanted to do was establish a foundation with my trust fund. So I did, and I made its primary focus a medical-assistance program in Honduras. For over a year I've done a lot of traveling, recruiting volunteers who are willing to spend a week or two fighting disease and related problems there."

His posture hadn't relaxed, but he was looking at her through different eyes than before. "That's what you do with all your time? Your money? Why I had such a hard time reaching you?"

"Right. My older brother, Alex, researches tropical diseases. He's based in Honduras with an international health organization. Together we've laid the groundwork for a constantly rotating crew of short-term volunteers who'll shuttle in and out. Soon our first team will make the inaugural trip. The first of many, we hope."

The Reluctant Bachelor

Jon's memory skipped back a day, lingered, and he winced as a sudden, painful tightness invaded his stomach. *A trip. Roughing it.* "You're going too, aren't you?"

"Yes," she whispered, clearly shocked by the harshness in his voice.

Jon was at a loss to explain why her announcement had caused such a gut reaction. Or why it seemed so imperative that he keep her from leaving.

"But you spent years there. Don't you already know enough about the place that you needn't go back?"

Cassy sent him a rueful smile. "I have a pretty good idea of what's in store for all of us. But after planning toward this for so long, I'm not about to miss the payoff."

It made perfect sense for her to want to be in Honduras for the start-up of a program that represented a massive undertaking on her part. Yet the thought of her going disturbed him, and he wasn't sure why. "Isn't your work on this end—finding people—more important than anything you can do down there?" That rationale sounded lame, even to him.

"Well, naturally, the recruiting will continue. But it'll have to wait until I see that everything is running smoothly in Honduras. Too much is at stake to take a chance on any last-minute snafus."

He faced her, wanting to argue further, knowing anything he said would make him seem petty and unreasonable. He'd just have to find another means of convincing her to stay in Houston. After all, he had weeks before she left. In the meantime, he had some fence-mending to do. "It appears I've made a lot of wrong assumptions about you."

Cassy grinned, relieved that he'd quickly given up trying to convince her that she shouldn't go to Honduras. She swept her braid behind her. "I'm more interested in how you plan to atone for misjudging me."

She saw his shoulders straighten, his eyes narrow and darken. "First, I think I'll kiss you speechless. How does that sound for openers?"

"Impossible, with you across the room."

He advanced slowly, his intent strengthening with each step. No longer relaxed, Cassy closed her eyes, willing him to hurry. She felt the couch accept his weight, felt the heat of him as he bent over her, and at last, the sweet invasion of his tongue as it slipped into her mouth.

Her senses came alive as his tongue swept over and under hers. She felt the prickle of incipient whiskers as his mouth moved in a slow glide along her jaw, down her neck, over her exposed collarbones.

Cassy gasped as he left a trail of kisses along the sensitive flesh just above the elastic of her strapless dress. Her breasts were full and aching, needing the warm pressure of his hands. She arched against him, a breathless, silent plea to be touched. The moist tip of his tongue worked beneath the edge of the thin cotton, and Cassy bit her lip to keep from crying out.

Jon's hand climbed upward with agonizing slowness. But as his palm closed over her breast, she was wrenched from her sensual languor by the sound of the bolt turning in her front lock.

"What the hell—" Jon grated.

The Reluctant Bachelor

As they struggled to sit up, an astonished voice said, "Oops! Sorry. Don't mind me, Cass. I'll just leave the keys and let myself out. Y'all won't even know I've been here."

5

CASSY GROANED. The interruption was her own fault. Earlier that day she'd loaned Holly the Chrysler when her car wouldn't start. She had told her neighbor to use the spare apartment key and drop off the car keys when she returned from her tutoring session.

As Cassy detached herself and rearranged her clothes, she could feel resentment in every muscle of Jon's rigid form. "It's okay," she called to Holly's rapidly disappearing back. "Don't run off."

A slight figure emerged from the shadowy hall. Her gamine face and pixie haircut seemed at odds with the huge round glasses perched on the tip of her nose.

Eyeing Jonathan uneasily, Holly said, "I really am sorry about this, Cass. Honest. I never dreamed that you'd be in here with, uh, you know, a man." She took a couple of backward steps. "Thanks for letting me use your car. I'll talk to you in the morning."

Cassy and Jon listened in silence as the door snapped shut behind their unwelcome intruder.

"Friend of yours?" he asked. His thumb and index finger spanned from temple to temple, as if he had a headache.

Cassy would have preferred to take up right where they'd left off. But he had moved back to his chair and looked as if he meant to stay there. Stalking over to the temporary dining table, she mouthed a silent oath and started wadding up the cloth. Too many people and obligations were infringing on their time. She'd finally found the one man for her, and they couldn't get on with the business of falling in love because someone or something always interfered.

"I guess you could say she's actually more Meri's friend. That's how I met her. They used to be roommates, when they taught at the same school."

Jon looked skeptical. "And now she has keys to your apartment?"

"Well, she lives across the hall and sort of looks after things when I'm gone."

"In exchange for a cut in her rent?"

"It's to our mutual advantage," Cassy said defensively. It was nobody's business that she didn't charge Holly a dime of rent and occasionally paid her for doing extra odd jobs. Working your way through graduate school wasn't easy. "With me having to be away so much, it's a big relief to know I can rely on Holly to take care of anything that comes up."

"I'm sure it is." His voice softened. "I didn't mean to sound disapproving. Blame it on a terminal case of frustration." He propped one ankle on his opposite knee. "When I'm around you, nothing seems to go as I planned."

"You had plans for tonight?" Cassy again sat on the sofa, disgruntled but resigned that the romantic part of the evening had passed.

She could see him steeling himself, much as she had done minutes ago when she'd explained the foundation's work. "My main objective was asking you to reconsider the Aruba trip."

"But we've already agreed that you'd donate the cost of the trip to the Hunger Coalition."

"And I have. What I'm talking about is just between us. I know you said you have no intention of going, but think about it. This would be the perfect opportunity for us to get away from all these things that keep coming between us."

"Sounds wonderful." It sounded like heaven.

"Don't you see, between all your traveling and the commitments and responsibilities you have when you are here, there's no time left for us." He stood, as though being on his feet might make his argument more persuasive. "We both know something is happening between us. Or trying to. But we have to get away from all these distractions and give it a chance. We deserve that, and I want it."

"I want it, too," Cassy said in a plaintive voice. "If only I didn't have so much to do during the next couple of months." She ran down the list of items clogging her calendar, seeing his expression turn grimmer with each addition. "Then, we're talking Aruba. Who'd want to go to the tropics when it's hot as an inferno here?"

"Cassy, honey," he said, coming over to sit beside her. "Free up a week and leave the rest to me. I promise I'll find a place you'll like. Somewhere cool." He lifted her hand and nibbled on her fingertips as an incentive. "Is it a deal?"

His touch finally convinced her. Especially since that was what she'd wanted all along. "If I can free up a week, it's a deal." She'd have to move heaven and earth, but she'd beaten more overwhelming odds.

"Okay, call me when you get back to town. And that means before you leave again." He took her mouth in a fast, greedy kiss. "From now on, I need to know where you are. Every minute."

He looked almost as shocked to hear himself say that as Cassy was to hear it. After pondering for a bit, he looked at her with a glint of challenge in his eyes. "Presumptuous and chauvinistic, right?"

"Just a tad."

"So sue me."

JON HUNG UP THE PHONE feeling as excited as a man scheduling his honeymoon. The analogy gave him a moment's pause, but it didn't diminish the excitement. Marriage was an issue he had evaded, all the while maintaining he had no particular bias against it. Just that *he* wasn't suited for it. With Cassy, he'd taken his best shot at exercising the usual amount of caution. It hadn't done him a damn bit of good. His fascination with her had grown until it bordered on obsessive.

When she said she didn't want to go anywhere warm, he'd immediately pictured the ideal getaway spot for them. A few years back, Atlantis had been involved in a joint venture development in the Canadian Rockies. Jon had spent more time on site than he normally did and had fallen under the spell of the place. After the project was completed, he'd returned to the remote lodge often, immersing himself in the isolation. He always came back revived and inspired.

But for the first time, he wanted to share it.

That surprised Jon because, in many respects, he was a private person. Spending a certain amount of time by himself was almost a physical need. There were things he preferred to do alone—travel, shower, sleep. Now he wanted to do all of them with Cassy.

The only hitch in his flawless scenario would be if she couldn't set aside the time to go away with him. With a vicious yank, Jon pulled a folder from the stack of work that he'd put aside while arranging the details of their trip. He refused to even consider not having Cassy all to himself for a week. He wanted it too desperately. He needed it.

LATE THURSDAY AFTERNOON, Cassy pulled into the small lot behind the fourplex just as Meredith was parking her snazzy yellow compact. "You look disgustingly fresh," Cassy groused, dragging her canvas weekend bag from the back seat.

"Air conditioning is the secret, dearest, as I've told you many times. Really, Cass, it's absurd that I, a poverty-ridden schoolteacher, drive a decent car while you, a Laurens, roast in that beater."

Normally, Cassy would have quoted how many units of vaccine could be purchased for the cost of a new car. Today it was too hot to wear a crusader's cape. "Put a cork in the lectures. I'm wiped out. All I want is a cool shower and a phone, not necessarily in that order." She didn't protest when Meri relieved her of the suitcase.

"Who are you so eager to call? Could it be...the hunk?"

"Every male over twenty and under eighty is a hunk to you," Cassy teased. She unlocked her door, grateful for the cool air, despite its mustiness. "Are you referring to one in particular?"

Meredith bypassed her own apartment, followed Cassy in and fixed them both a cold drink before flopping down on the sofa. "I like Jon, Cass. He's a bit too sedate and reserved for my taste, but that's of no consequence. He's yours, and I think he'll suit you nicely."

"I promised to call him the minute I got home. I've been shifting everything around so we can go away for a week."

"This sounds serious. Already?"

"Yes, already." Serious enough that Cassy had squeezed a doctor's appointment into her busy schedule. Children were definitely a part of her future, but in the meantime, she intended to assume the responsibility of birth control.

She inched Meri toward the door, telling her about Jon's promise to come up with a vacation spot that would be cool. Sharing a confidence was the least she could do in return for being so inhospitable.

"Well, I'm glad to see you finally doing something constructive about your love life, Cass. Lord knows it's been sadly lacking. I was getting concerned."

Cassy laughed at her friend's parting words. "I'll talk to you before I leave tomorrow," she said, closing the door.

A little breathless, she reached for the phone. She could wait a while longer for her refreshing shower.

Thirty minutes later she needed its cooling effects even more. Jon had been devilishly unrestrained in his welcome-back words. So frank, in fact, that he'd had her squirming in the chair. Even more exhilarating was his announcement that he'd been thinking all week about her going to the hill country alone in that rattletrap car.

On the verge of informing him that she and the Chrysler had covered thousands of miles without mishap, Cassy clapped her mouth shut when he proposed his alternative plan. If she'd delay departure a few hours until he could get away from his office, he wanted to drive her. It didn't sound like a casual offer. It sounded insistent.

Jon had advanced to this point relatively quickly. She wasn't about to argue over anything so trifling as what time she left. Gabe had said it didn't matter when she got there, and Jon's suggestion meant another chance to be with him. Of course, it also meant another call to Gabe. He sounded like his old self on the phone, but the good spirits could be a front. She felt reassured when he insisted that it was fine to bring Jonathan, that he had so many spare bedrooms they could each have two. Then he'd added the sly innuendo, "Or share one." That sounded like the Gabe she'd known all her life.

CASSY'D BARELY BEEN ABLE to stand the wait. She was so eager to see Jon that she had the door open almost before he could knock. He didn't waste time with a greeting, letting the embrace of his arms and the thrilling play of his mouth articulate better than words how glad he was to see her.

"I missed you, too," she said shakily, wanting to kiss him more yet needing to talk to him, too.

His strong hold on her didn't ease. If anything, it tightened. "God, Cassy, I thought Friday would never get here. For the next couple of days I don't want to think about you going *anywhere*."

Eyes alight, she drew back far enough to see his face. "Nowhere?" she asked, feeling excited and playful. "Not even, say, a week from tomorrow, to a destination of your choice?"

The Reluctant Bachelor

He went very still, then the light in his eyes matched hers. "You mean it? You can really go? For a whole week?"

Cassy nodded, grinning. It pleased her that Jonathan looked as if she had given him the best news of his life. Now she was glad she'd waited to tell him in person. "Is the week after next good for you? I mean, can you arrange things on that short notice?"

He looked a bit sheepish, then chuckled. "Last Monday I made reservations for the next eight weeks. Figured I had all the bases pretty well covered that way."

"Until yesterday, I still wasn't sure that I could make everything fit into my time limit and other people's schedules. You must have had more confidence in my juggling ability than I did."

"I just refused to consider that our trip wouldn't work out. I wanted it too much." His hands rested lightly on her shoulders, and his expression was earnest. "Cassy, I want to keep the details a surprise, but I'll make sure you won't regret this."

"How could I, Jon? Our time together is too hard to come by... and too special for regrets."

She saw him swallow, watched his mouth lower to hers for a kiss so tender, so cherishing, it filled her with emotions that were powerful and new and precious. But that was only the beginning, as the intent of their kiss gradually altered, becoming deeper and unbearably tempting. When he at last let go of her, Cassy couldn't recall where they were, much less where they were supposed to go.

Later that afternoon, speeding along the Katy Freeway, she told herself to sit across the car from him and be calm, as if his kiss hadn't practically melted her molars. But after nearly an hour, vibrations still pulsed deeply inside her.

She also cautioned herself that they weren't lovers stealing away for a romantic weekend tryst. She was on an important mission that had nothing to do with Jonathan. When a little bell sounded in her head, Cassy toyed with the possibilities and came to a wondrous conclusion. Why hadn't she seen the absolute perfection of it before? This trip had everything to do with her and Jon's future. Provided she could convert Gabe to the cause.

Fate had smiled on her again, and she hadn't even realized it....

They stopped in Schulenburg for barbecue, a taste Cassy had acquired since moving to her adopted state. Good thing, too, because Jon, a native Houstonian, said he grew up eating it at least once a week. She filed that away for future reference, treasuring even the trivial details she learned about him.

It was past ten o'clock and raining when they headed northwest from San Antonio to Kerrville and the hill country. They still had quite a distance to go. She hoped Gabe didn't go to bed early, although it would serve him right if they woke him up. He'd been so pigheaded about agreeing on a time. According to him, he didn't own a watch or clock and wasn't into schedules these days. Gabriel Coltrane had many things to recommend him, but belying his virtues was a vein of pure cussedness that would try a saint's patience.

Then again, he might be her good-news angel.

She and Jon talked easily the rest of the way, but what she had to accomplish lingered in her consciousness, growing in importance with every mile.

The Reluctant Bachelor 93

They cruised by the Kerrville city limits sign, and he asked, "Do you know the way from here?"

"Only that we have to go on to Ingram and then call him."

"'Him'?"

Cassy glanced over when she heard the edge in Jon's one-word question. "Him. Gabriel, the friend we're going to visit."

"I see."

She couldn't believe Jon would find anything wrong with her friendship with Gabe. "Gabe said his place is so secluded he'd never be able to give me directions. That's the reason I'm supposed to call. So he can come lead us to his house."

"I see."

The phrase was the same, only its edge had been honed. "He's been playing hermit on the hill for the past few years. Only within the past three months did he get a phone so anyone could reach him."

"I see."

Jonathan displaying a machismo mentality came out of left field. She couldn't let it pass unchallenged. "I can handle the conversation on my own from this point," she chided. "I'll say something, then fill in 'I see' for your part. You won't even have to listen or open your mouth."

"Sometimes, Cassy," he said, enunciating each syllable, "you need to understand that it isn't wise to poke a tiger."

The reference was oblique, but she got the message. "Gabriel and I have known each other since we wore diapers. Our parents are best friends. Being physically attracted to each other would seem incestuous."

"Maybe," he said, sounding calm. But his hands tightened on the wheel. "And maybe I'm just thinking about what I'd do if I had you alone for a night on a secluded hilltop."

She'd had plenty of thoughts along those lines herself. "Believe me, Gabe and I could sleep in the same bed and, between us, not be able to conjure up an amorous fantasy involving each other."

"My mind is full of them, and I don't even have to be in the same *state* with you."

Besieged by vivid mental images, Cassy leaned back and let them unfold inside her head until Jon swerved into a darkened service station parking lot. "There's a phone booth. Better make the call before I turn around and drag you off to that motel we passed a way back."

He always looked stunned when he blurted out statements like that. And Cassy was always delighted to be the one who inspired him to forget his restraint.

She fumbled through her purse, searching for glasses and the small notebook in which she'd jotted down Gabe's number. She couldn't find either. Missing glasses were nothing new, but Cassy never went anywhere without the notebook. She used it to keep track of the countless details in her complicated life. Then she remembered. They were both on her desk, by the phone. Where Jon had kissed her. She must have gotten so carried away that she forgot them. If this kept up, soon they'd both be incapable of rational action. She blinked and shifted her gaze to the droplet-covered side window.

The phone booth was an old-fashioned freestanding type, the kind rarely seen in cities these days, and Jon had parked as close to it as he could. Cassy scrambled from the car, braving the rain to dash the remaining distance. When she closed the bifold door, a light came on. The booth was also equipped with a directory, another convenience one didn't usually find in the city. Apparently ripping off phone books wasn't a big sport in small towns. Nor was staying up late. As far as she could see, the few distant streetlights illuminated no sign of activity.

It was going to be iffy reading the small print without her magnifiers. "Impossible," she muttered after opening the book. She couldn't hold the directory far enough away inside the cramped enclosure, so Cassy opened the door to extend her arms, but then the light shut off. Not only couldn't she see the print, she could barely make out the book, and it was getting soaked in the bargain.

Undaunted, she reversed positions, standing in the rain with water pelting her while she maneuvered the door closed far enough to activate the light. This would work if she could figure out how to turn pages one-handed.

"What in hell are you doing?" Jon plastered himself to her back, simultaneously yanking aside the door and propelling both of them inside the booth.

It was a tight fit; the air around them loomed heavy and damp. His nearness was stimulating, giving her ideas that were inappropriate, if not impossible, in a phone booth. She put them aside and patiently explained what she'd been trying to do.

He plunked a coin in the slot and dialed directory assistance. "What's Gabe's last name?" She told him, he requested and memorized the number before punching buttons and handing her the receiver.

After a short conversation, Cassy said, "It'll take him about twenty minutes to get here, maybe longer in this weather."

"Mmm." It was steamy inside the small enclosure, and Jon's avid gaze moved over her upturned face. "You have raindrops on your lashes."

The pad of his little finger skimmed lightly over the dark brown tips, and Cassy's eyes closed involuntarily.

"And here."

His palms framed her neck, and he bent to her ear. She moaned as his tongue faithfully defined each dip and whorl, licking up the drops of moisture, then covering the rest of her face with the same prolonged, sensual stroking. Breath lodged in Cassy's throat, and electric sensations coursed through her.

"Your mouth is wet, too. And I can't resist it."

Cassy's arms slid around his waist, and she fitted herself against him. She willingly offered her mouth and anything else he would demand. Her soft sound of acquiescence was muffled by the slant of his lips over hers. He kissed her deeply, the intimate caress of his tongue filling, promising, making her burn. Her nails sank into his back, urging him closer. At the mild punishment, he threw back his head and sucked in a deep breath. But his hips remained pressed to hers, rocking gently.

"Jon, I don't think I can stand much more of this."

"I know," he whispered roughly, levering himself away from her. "I promise myself I'm not going to start something that can't be finished, and then every time I get within ten feet of you, it's like pouring gasoline on a blaze."

"Gabe won't care if we share a room," she said, need making her bold and reckless.

He exhaled audibly and planted one hand high on the side of the booth. "Wanting you is torture, but I have plans for our first time together. Atmosphere that will enhance the mood. We'll take our time and draw out the pleasure until we're wild to have each other. And privacy. Because, Cassy, I'm not going to love you quietly."

She melted against the hard length of him, weak and tremulous from just the words. What would it be like when he delivered on those inflaming promises? "Talk about pouring gasoline on a blaze," she murmured, rubbing her cheek over his damp shirtfront.

"Lord," he groaned, "I can't stop, Cassy." His fingers found the top button of her blouse, and she could feel them shaking.

She reached to steady them, flattening his hands over the slope of her breasts, pressing lightly. He squeezed, a gentle contrast to the possessive way he was devouring her mouth, and she hoped he'd never stop. Cassy jumped and Jon froze when a pair of high-beam lights further illuminated their lovers' clinch.

His curse was short but emphatic. "This just proves what I've been saying all along. I can't even get you to myself in a phone booth out here in the boondocks."

They got back into the car, relinquishing their spot to a teenage couple, whose smirks and sidelong glances conveyed that people as old as Jon and Cassy ought to be past smooching in phone booths.

"Why would someone who was raised on a lake in Minnesota hide out on a hill in Texas?"

Jon's question sounded very casual, but Cassy sensed his curiosity about Gabe was real. "You already know that Gabe and I grew up together. But we also joined the Peace Corps at the same time."

"Noblesse oblige."

A few weeks ago she'd have interpreted that remark as a slap at her privileged upbringing. Now it sounded faintly admiring. "If you want to know the truth, Gabe's always been much more acquisitive than anyone in my family. Probably because Coltrane money has been around longer than dirt."

"Whereas Cassidy and Laurens wealth is only two generations old?"

"Something like that, I guess. We haven't learned how to be comfortably rich." This was a conversation that they couldn't have had at their first meeting. "But I'm not about to be critical. Gabe's earned the luxury of his hilltop hideout the hard way."

Jon turned in his seat. "What do you mean?"

Cassy summarized the story in a monotone. "During the final year of his second tour in Central America, Gabe and another PCV were 'detained for questioning' by one of those fanatical guerrilla groups terrorizing that part of the world."

"He was kidnapped? A prisoner?"

"Oh, yes. And it ultimately turned into an even nastier incident."

"Couldn't the government do something in a case like that?" Jon asked indignantly.

"Not when they're trying to intervene covertly while maintaining a policy of not negotiating with terrorists." Cassy had been in another country at the time, but she'd never forget the tension that mounted daily. "His captors loved the international television exposure, even though the Coltranes were able to keep the networks from naming names."

"I remember now. They kept referring to him as the heir to a substantial American fortune, as though that were both the cause and solution to his plight."

"Exactly," Cassy whispered, recalling the weeks of frustration and fear. "If Gabe's family had been penniless, the guerrillas would have dealt with U.S. representatives. As it was, the Coltranes finally sent in a contingent of mercenaries. Very select. Very expensive. They freed both of the captives."

It had stopped raining and storm clouds were moving rapidly toward the east. Jon took one of Cassy's balled fists. "Was that when Gabe headed for the hills?"

"Yes. He disappeared after the requisite State Department debriefing. Tonight will be the first time I've seen him, although he contacted me to set up his convoluted communication system. Until he got a phone, I had to call his nearest neighbor who would then deliver my message."

"You mean you've known how to get in touch with him, but not where he is?"

"Right. If I deemed it a genuine emergency, I could notify him. But I've decided that it's time for him to come out of hiding. He's got too much going for him to be a hermit forever."

She told Jon about Gabriel's impressive wilderness skills, his phenomenal ability to work with people and meld them into a cohesive team, his widespread network of contacts. "The kind of person to have on your side in any situation," she said.

The man sounded like a damned saint, Jon thought morosely. No, his namesake was an angel. He only half listened when she launched into yet another tribute. He wasn't panting to meet this paragon, but it was better than hearing Cassy sing his praises.

With idle interest he watched a four-wheel-drive pickup careen into the parking lot and churn up a wake as it plowed toward them. The mud-spattered monster jerked to a halt close to his door. Jon noted with some small satisfaction that the angel had chosen an unremarkable vehicle to herald his arrival.

And he didn't look at all angelic. In fact, Jon thought as the man climbed out of his truck, he resembled a younger, slimmer Grizzly Adams. Unruly gold-streaked brown hair flirted with his shoulders, and a dark beard obscured most of his face. Jon switched on the key to lower his window.

"Gabe Coltrane. Good to meet you," he drawled, bending his considerable height to poke a hand through the open window.

Jon glanced at the hand as he shook it, found it tan, strong and callused, as if Gabe labored outdoors. "Jonathan Manning," Jon answered, surprised to find himself warming instantly to the affable mountain man he'd been maligning seconds before.

"Lookin' good, Cass," he said with a wink as she jumped out of the car and embraced him. "Texans must agree with you."

She passed over the teasing remark. "And you, Gabe, look, um, interesting. But then you always did get totally immersed in whatever cause you embrace. By the way, the twang is pretty good. You've obviously been practicing."

Jon studied the two while they traded banter laced with barbs. On the lookout for signs of more between them than Cassy had claimed, he saw mutual affection and an easiness that came from a long-standing acquaintance. But he didn't pick up any undercurrents of the kind he'd been secretly dreading. She had been straight about her relationship with Gabe, and Jon felt relief begin to dissolve the knot in his midsection. He guessed his unease might be attributed to not understanding how any man could know Cassy and not be enthralled by her. In every way.

They followed the big truck out of town on the main highway before turning onto a winding secondary route. After three more turns, Jon pulled onto a mud-slickened dirt road and cringed. His car was going to be every bit as filthy as the four-wheel drive. The things a man would suffer in the name of love.

Love! He felt sweat pop out on his forehead, and a peculiar sensation tightened his stomach. Just a figure of speech, he assured himself. He liked Cassy, found her interesting, admired what she did. Desired her. But love? That simply wasn't possible. It didn't happen this quickly.

Weaving, skidding, they traversed one of the hills after which the region was named. "Not exactly my definition of a hermit's hovel," Jon commented, surveying the large, native-stone house that rambled over the summit.

"He can live in a palace for the rest of his life, and I won't care." Cassy sprinted from the car onto a stone and cedar porch, meeting Gabe. They turned to motion Jon in, then arm in arm entered the house. He gathered their bags and followed the pair inside.

Cassy and Gabe spent the next hour bringing each other up-to-date with news of family and friends. She was careful to include Jon, explaining who was whom and adding tidbits of information or anecdotes so he could share in their enjoyment of the stories.

When they finally ran down, Gabe pointed Cassy and Jon toward a long wing with four doors opening off it. "I'll leave the choice of rooms to you." Over his shoulder, he tacked on, "Oh, in case you're interested, I get up early now that I'm a man of the land."

Jon leaned against a wall, watching Cassy open each door and peer inside. She selected the last room and came back to pick up her suitcase. In front of her door, she turned to face him. "Jonathan, when we're on the trip, alone..."

"I'll be lucky to survive that long." She seemed to be seeking silent confirmation of what was on both their minds, and he was eager to give it. "Everything will be different then, Cassy." The hall clock's tick was abnormally loud, in time with the blood pulsing through Jon's body. It was tying him in knots to not go after her. But as he'd said earlier, he wanted everything perfect. This wasn't the time or place.

He said, "See you in the morning," and ducked through the nearest door. Not that it mattered where he went. He probably didn't stand a chance of sleeping a wink.

Without realizing it, Cassy had chosen a room facing east. She'd stayed awake a long time wishing on stars dotting the black sky beyond a glass expanse that formed the exterior wall. It was so dark here, so quiet, so far removed from civilization. She felt secure, happy and expectant, much as she had as a child when her family went to their summer cottage in northern Minnesota.

Awakened early by the sun, she stretched and hugged her pillow. How would she be feeling if Jon had cast aside his good intentions and joined her in the big bed? Even better, she decided, making her way to the bathroom.

Cassy showered quickly, braided her hair wet and pulled on khaki walking shorts and a safari shirt. She found Gabe on the patio with an array of tomahawks spread before him on a silvered cedar picnic table. "Thought you and Jon might sleep in," he said, absorbed with the task of honing the edge of an already wicked-looking iron head.

She took in the magnificent panorama of Gabe's hilltop. A misty blanket veiled the lower terrain, leaving only the sun-washed crests clearly visible. "As you know, I've always been an early riser. I don't know anything about Jonathan's sleeping habits."

"But you'd like to?"

"Before long, I will."

"So it's serious between the two of you?"

"Getting there. Not soon enough for me. Too fast for him, I think." Cassy filled Gabe in on how they'd met, her feelings for Jon and his inborn caution against rushing into anything intense. "I just wish he could stop resisting, see how right this is."

"You could look at it another way. Knowing he's not quick to leap into relationships probably means that once he does, he'll be a hundred percent committed to it."

Smiling, Cassy picked up one of the hatchetlike weapons and tested the weight and grip. "Ever since we were kids, you've always known what to say to make me feel better." She paused, waiting for him to look at her. When he did, her face was somber. "That's why I'm here. To ask for your help, Gabe. It's the most important favor I'll ever ask of anybody."

6

GABE SET HIS TOMAHAWK DOWN very carefully and wiped his hands on a cloth. "I knew it had to be something pretty heavy when you called and asked to come over here."

Cassy touched his arm. "Gabriel, the last three years I've respected your need for solitude. I've never told anyone where you are, in spite of some powerful pressure. Only when your father was so ill did I contact you. But it's been hell on me because I care, and I wanted to help. I love you like a brother. When you hurt, so do I."

"Which is the reason I picked you as the one person who knew how to find me. I trusted you to understand and not betray my confidence whether or not you agreed with my choice of therapy."

She hadn't agreed at all, fearing he'd needed extensive professional help. But Gabe had been adamant about going into hiding, insisting he would heal himself. She swallowed to relieve the dryness in her mouth, oddly hesitant to ask the crucial question. "Did the isolation work?"

He flashed her a grin, white teeth looking very wolfish amidst the beard. "What do you think?"

Cassy matched his grin. He certainly seemed like the Gabe she'd grown up with. "Does that mean you're ready to reenter the outside world?" she asked, optimism building.

"Well, I hate to break this to you, but I've been reentered for a couple of years now. It's just a different world than I used to live in."

She listened in awe as he rattled off a list of unique new skills he'd acquired, volunteer work he'd done with Scouts and school classes, and most bizarre of all, digging up stumps on his property for fun and profit.

"You support yourself selling stumps?"

He laughed. "I never claimed that. I don't share your guilt about spending inherited wealth. Every quarter, when that big old check is deposited in my account, I get a big old smile. Then I buy some more land. You ought to try it sometime."

"My money is tied up in the foundation. I only take expenses and a token salary."

"I admire what you're using your money for in Honduras, Cass. But let's face it, I've always been into status symbols a lot more than you. I like having things and suffer no guilt for taking advantage of my wealth."

"Right. I don't have to raise the garage door to know there's at least one Ferrari parked beside that filthy pickup truck. But don't you sometimes feel the old idealism urging you to do something more?"

The first time Gabe had called her in Houston, she'd outlined the objectives of her plan to him. Now she was going to appeal to him on an emotional level. "You know how people exist down there. You've seen them, and that kind of misery is preventable."

"Hey, you don't have to convince me that your aims are noble and good. But, Cass, I learned one thing during that time when every day looked as if it might be my last. And that was, you can't save the world."

Cassy studied his stark features. This was the first time he'd mentioned anything at all about being held captive. "I have no delusions about saving the world. All I want to do is provide immunizations and some basic medical care to people who're victims of a cruel cycle of hunger and disease. You can help me do it. I need you."

"You know I'd do most anything for you. Just, please, don't ask me to go back to that part of the world." He got up from the picnic table and paced. It was the first sign of agitation she'd seen in the habitually laid-back Gabe. "My head's on straight now—no nightmares, no hang-ups. But this hilltop is about as far south as I ever intend to venture."

"That's the beauty of my proposition. You'll never have to set foot outside the U.S.A."

"You want a donation? How much?"

Cassy smiled. "Contributions are always welcome, of course. But I have something a bit more active in mind."

"Okay," he said with a sigh. "Tell me how I can do my part without leaving the country."

"As you know, I've been traveling almost constantly for over a year. Recruiting volunteers, lots of them, is crucial to the success of our project in Honduras, and doing it face-to-face is the most effective means of convincing people to join us."

Gabe sprawled into a patio chair and propped up his moccasined feet. "So you decided to try the pitch on me?"

"Something like that," she admitted, glancing toward the house. "Since I met Jonathan, being away so much has really created problems. My work is so important to me, so necessary, but I—"

"Want to be with him all the time?"

"Is mind reading another of your new talents?"

"Nope, but I'd have to be pretty thick not to see how you look at the guy. Or to figure out my role in your plan. You want me to take over the recruiting for you, right?"

"You're a natural for this, Gabe. You can sweet-talk anybody into anything."

"I think *I've* been sweet-talked," he grumbled. His tone was full of indulgent amusement, but his demeanor remained somber. "I can't give you any promises yet. What you want entails a big step for me, and I'll have to think about it. But, Cass, I'll think very hard."

"Oh, thank you." She rushed over and bent to give him a hug and a huge kiss on the cheek. "I know you won't let me down." She had to believe that. Otherwise she and Jon might not be guaranteed happily ever after.

Cassy had never met a more capable or obstinate person than Gabriel Coltrane. Whatever he made up his mind to do, he persisted until it was accomplished. If he took on the task of traveling the country to recruit volunteers in her stead, before he was finished, there'd be a waiting list. Relieved of that time-consuming responsibility, Cassy could devote herself to creating and implementing more effective ways to accomplish their objectives. But equally important was the added time she'd have with Jonathan.

At last she allowed herself a sigh of relief. Her business with Gabe was completed. She could relax and enjoy the rest of their visit.

HANDS RAMMED in his pockets, Jon stood at a window watching Cassy and Gabe out on the patio. He didn't want to join them until he got a handle on his restless, edgy mood. That was going to be difficult considering what had caused the uneasiness.

Last night, unable to sleep, he'd replayed Cassy's account of Gabe's ordeal with the terrorists. It made his skin crawl and his gut churn. He had recognized his reaction as fear. Fear for Cassy's safety in a region of the world where kidnapping was an accepted fact of life.

He had tried hard to understand her dedication to her work. Yet from the moment she told him she'd be going to Honduras, his brain had screamed silently, "No, I can't let you," although his motives had been vague and undefined.

At first he'd chastised himself for being unreasonable, even selfish. Maybe he had been. He couldn't deny that, given a choice, he'd prefer her staying close to him. But that seemed insignificant compared to the real threat.

In Central America, Cassy was a prime target to be kidnapped. Tortured. Maybe even... No! He couldn't allow himself to dwell on what might happen. And he couldn't allow her to take such a risk. Somehow he had to convince her not to go to Honduras. Which would probably be about as easy as getting rid of the knot in his stomach that had kept him awake most of last night.

The two on the patio had stopped their animated discussion, and both looked solemn. Then Cassy swarmed all over Gabe. Just a hug and kiss between old friends, nothing really to provoke jealousy, Jon told himself. He'd just rather that she be kissing him with such enthusiasm. He smiled, remembering all the times she'd done just that.

Cassy's outburst must mean that she had gotten her wish. On the way from Houston, she'd said the trip was to ask for Gabe's help. She'd held up crossed fingers on both hands, whispering that if she breathed a word about the details, then her wish wouldn't come true. He'd teased her about being superstitious, but she remained unmoved. Jon had assumed she was after a big contribution, though. What else could it be? Gabe's self-imposed exile precluded him actually serving as one of Cassy's volunteers. Who could blame the man for wanting never to go back after his last experience in that part of the world? Maybe Jon could even enlist Gabe's help in dissuading Cassy.

Encouraged that he'd at last come up with a rational argument against the trip, he was able to greet her and Gabe with a smile that wasn't too forced.

ON THE DRIVE back to Houston on Sunday afternoon, Jon pondered the best way to broach his concerns about her Honduras trip without sounding like an irrational alarmist. Finally he just plunged ahead. "Cassy, it seems to me you should reconsider the risks of going to such a dangerous place."

"You mean Honduras? Dangerous?" She was silent for a moment, then apparently picked up on his line of thinking. "Oh, you mean in light of what I told you about Gabe. You can't really compare our situations.

He was in another country with a totally different political climate, and that did happen some time ago."

"I don't think Central America has become a model of stability in the intervening years." He glanced over, holding her gaze for a few seconds.

"But that was a fluke—"

"That might happen again. Doesn't your family remember what the Coltranes went through? I'd think they would want to protect you from anything like that." At a time when it was important to defend his position calmly and reasonably, his emotions were threatening to take over. *He* wanted to protect her.

Very quietly, Cassy said, "My family raised us to not be afraid of doing what we think is necessary. My mother marched for civil rights in the sixties and later for nuclear disarmament. As she says, right and safe don't always go hand in hand."

She reached over and touched his arm. "I appreciate your concern, Jon. But really, you needn't worry about me."

Jon didn't say anything. He didn't trust himself not to shout. *Concern!* What a wimpy way to express how he felt about Cassy. He damned sure knew it was more than concern. He also knew the subject was closed for today. And when she started talking in that sexy voice of hers about how much she was looking forward to their going away together in six days, all thoughts of Honduras went up in smoke.

When they got back to her apartment, he didn't want to leave her, but he had no choice. In less than an hour, she was expecting twenty medical students from Baylor, who, with a little persuasion, would make excellent volunteers.

His only consolation was that soon he'd have her all to himself.

CASSY OPENED HER DOOR to an insistent summons early Friday morning. Meredith sailed in wearing a paisley shirtwaist and a stubbornly set jaw. It was her "issuing orders" expression. She slapped a briefcase down on the cluttered dining table.

"Why aren't you dressed?" she demanded, frowning at Cassy's oversize yellow T-shirt and bare feet.

"Why aren't you at school?"

"I took a personal leave day to help you get ready."

Cassy yawned, suffering from abnormal morning sluggishness. She hadn't gotten home from the Rio Grande Valley until almost one, and at Jon's orders, called him the minute she arrived. They'd talked for more than an hour. "You're here to do the laundry and pack my suitcase?"

Meri didn't dignify the impudent question. She pawed around in the briefcase and pulled out a single sheet of paper, waving it in front of Cassy's nose. "Now, I want you to sign this oath."

She knew her head was muzzy from too little sleep, but Meri wasn't making sense. She eased herself into the chair across from her friend. After scrabbling through piles of debris littering her table, she gave up the search for her glasses. "What are you talking about? What oath?"

"Nothing to it," Meri said, handing her a pen. "You just swear you won't pack a single pair of white cotton panties when you go away with Jonathan."

Cassy broke up at Meri's mock-seriousness. "You must stay awake nights to come up with such outra-

THE JOKER GOES WILD!

Play this card right!

See inside!

HARLEQUIN WANTS TO GIVE YOU

- 4 free books
- A free bracelet watch
- A free mystery gift

IT'S A WILD, WILD, WONDERFUL
FREE OFFER!

HERE'S WHAT YOU GET:

1. *Four New Harlequin Temptation® Novels—FREE!* Everything comes up hearts and diamonds with four exciting romances—yours FREE from Harlequin Reader Service®. Each of these brand-new novels brings you the passion and tenderness of today's greatest love stories.

2. *A Practical and Elegant Bracelet Watch—FREE!* As a free gift simply to thank you for accepting four free books, we'll send yo a stylish bracelet watch. This classic LCD quartz watch is a perfect expression of your style and good taste, and it's yours FREE as an added thanks for giving our Reader Service a try.

3. *An Exciting Mystery Bonus—FREE!* You'll go wild over this surprise gift. It is attractive as well as practical.

4. *Money-Saving Home Delivery!* Join Harlequin Reader Service and enjoy the convenience of previewing 4 new books every month, delivered to your home. Each book is yours for $2.39* 26¢ less per book than the cover price. And there is *no* extra charge for postage and handling. If you're not fully satisfied, y can cancel at any time just by sending us a note or a shipping statement marked "cancel" or by returning any shipment to us our cost. Great savings and total convenience are the name of game at Harlequin!

5. *Free Newsletter!* It makes you feel like a partner to the world's most popular authors...tells about their upcoming books...even gives you their recipes!

6. *More Mystery Gifts Throughout the Year!* No joke! Because ho subscribers are our most valued readers, we'll be sending you additional free gifts from time to time with your monthly shipments—as a token of our appreciation!

GO WILD
WITH HARLEQUIN TODAY—
JUST COMPLETE, DETACH AND
MAIL YOUR FREE-OFFER CARD!

*Terms and prices subject to change without notice. N.Y. and Iowa residents subject to sales tax
© 1989 HARLEQUIN ENTERPRISES LTD.

GET YOUR GIFTS FROM HARLEQUIN
ABSOLUTELY FREE!

Mail this card today!

© 1989 HARLEQUIN ENTERPRISES LTD.

PRINTED IN U.S.A.

PLACE JOKER STICKER HERE

PLAY THIS CARD RIGHT!

YES! Please send me my 4 Harlequin Temptation® novels FREE along with my free Bracelet Watch and free mystery gift. I wish to receive all the benefits of the Harlequin Reader Service® as explained on the opposite page.

(U-H-T-10/89) 142 CIH MDVZ

NAME _____
(PLEASE PRINT)

ADDRESS _____ APT. ____

CITY _____

STATE _____ ZIP CODE _____

Offer limited to one per household and not valid for current Harlequin Temptation® subscribers. All orders subject to approval.

HARLEQUIN READER SERVICE® "NO RISK" GUARANTEE

- There's no obligation to buy—and the free books remain yours to keep.
- You pay the low members-only price and receive books before they appear in stores.
- You may end your subscription anytime—just write and let us know or return any shipment to us at our cost.

IT'S NO JOKE!
MAIL THE POSTPAID CARD INSIDE AND GET FREE GIFTS AND $10.60 WORTH OF HARLEQUIN NOVELS — *FREE!*

BUSINESS REPLY MAIL
FIRST CLASS   PERMIT NO. 717   BUFFALO, NY

POSTAGE WILL BE PAID BY ADDRESSEE

HARLEQUIN READER SERVICE
901 FUHRMANN BLVD
PO BOX 1867
BUFFALO NY 14240-9952

NO POSTAGE
NECESSARY
IF MAILED
IN THE
UNITED STATES

If offer card is missing, write to: Harlequin Reader Service, P.O. Box 1867, Buffalo, NY 14240 geous ideas. Why would I sign anything so ridiculous? Why would you care?"

"Because you need an adviser, dear heart. Cass, we're not dealing with summer camp, here. I cannot allow you to wear those prim little undies for an assignation. I think it's illegal."

"Also immaterial," Cassy added cheerfully. "You know I'm allergic to synthetics and can't wear those unmentionables you're always slinking around in."

"So wear silk. That's natural."

"Costs a fortune."

"Which you have," Meri countered, jabbing the air with her index fingers. "I promise, it won't be painful at all if you cut loose with a few of your zillions."

"How many zeroes are there in a zillion? I don't think I have nearly that much." Cassy knew that for every argument Meri would have a rebuttal. To be honest, the image of herself standing before Jon in seductive clothes was almost irresistible.

Smelling victory, Meri delivered her coup de grace. "Nothing compares to the feel of silk against you. Unless it's a man's skin."

Cassy yielded to her indisputable logic and went to get dressed.

THE JET HAD JUST TOUCHED DOWN in Calgary and moved onto the taxiway. They rolled past an oil well, the grasshopper pump mechanism modified to look like a horse. Astride it, a smiling wooden cowboy waved his welcome. Cassy snapped a couple of pictures, then turned to give Jon a peck on the cheek. "What a marvelous idea for our getaway! How did you think of it?"

He smiled, obviously pleased by her enthusiasm. "When you said you wanted cool, I immediately thought of here. We'll be going to one of my favorite places."

"We're not staying in Calgary?"

"No. It's a nice enough city, but..." He shrugged. "I wanted to take you somewhere special. Peaceful and remote. I think you'll like where I picked."

"I'm sure I will." Cassy had a whole week alone with Jon. That qualified as special enough. Still she was thrilled that he'd put so much effort into selecting their hideaway.

They cleared customs with little formality, claimed a rental car and left Calgary behind. The city was fairly flat, but she could soon see muted outlines of the Rockies. As they drove farther west, the mountains became more defined, majestic as they rose to pierce the clouds. Last winter's snow clung to the highest peaks and shaded lower areas. Within weeks, perhaps days, a new season's snowfall would begin. Small jewellike lakes popped into view frequently, their colors ranging from the palest azure to deep green.

Outside of Lake Louise, Jon drew Cassy's attention to a large wedge-shaped expanse that looked more like ice than snow. "The bluish cast is your clue to glaciers. Dust and rocks trapped inside give them their color."

"That's a first for me. Guess I thought they were all at the North Pole." She was getting dizzy looking from side to side. "There's so much to see, and everything is so spectacular. I can't take it all in."

"Don't try to. I've been here at least a dozen times and haven't come close to seeing it all." They passed a Yoho National Park sign. "There's a lot I want to show you, but sight-seeing can wait until tomorrow. Let's get settled at the lodge first so we can start to unwind."

"You're the guide," she said lightly. Her stomach rippled . . . and not from hunger.

A while later Jon stopped beside a small building and went to check in. Cassy looked around, anxious to see what sort of setting he'd picked. The parking lot was surrounded by tall trees, but there was no hint of a lodge. The solitude intrigued her, excited her. She rolled down her window and drew deeply of the clean, cool air.

The impending snow would make it even cooler and crisper. Pity she wouldn't be here to enjoy it. She'd be sweating in the tropics. Away from Jon. She banished that thought, determined not to let dread of being separated from him infringe on their week.

He came back shortly with their keys. "From here we can catch the shuttle, or if you feel like stretching your legs, we can walk. It's less than a mile. No cars are allowed on the property."

"How charming. I like it already. Let's walk." They set their luggage out to be picked up by the tractor-drawn baggage wagon, and Cassy changed to walking shoes.

They passed a horse concession, several marked trails, picnic spots and a canoe dock before reaching the weathered footbridge leading to the lodge. At that moment Cassy spotted the lake for the first time. It was a gorgeous little gem, a gleaming aquamarine edged with stately spruce and firs and cradled by towering peaks.

"It's lovely," she said breathlessly, awed by the glorious natural beauty of the place. "Thank you for sharing it with me."

Jon whispered and touched her lips with his. "My pleasure, Cassy."

Guests' accommodations were in four-unit timber-and-stone cottages that had been constructed to reflect the nineteenth century architecture of the original lodge. Their cottage was located on a point that boasted lake views from both front and side. Cassy was a bit disappointed, though not completely surprised, that she and Jon had the two upper units. He was adhering to the original terms of the trip—separate rooms.

No matter, she told herself with secret satisfaction. There were ways a woman could use privacy to her advantage....

After unpacking they walked over to the lodge's Kicking Horse Bar for a late lunch. Though the temperature was cool, they chose to sit outside on the deck.

"It's amazing," Cassy murmured, tilting her face to take advantage of the sun's gentle warmth. "The lure of a place like this is instantaneous. Five minutes after you arrive, you feel as though you've always been here and are meant to stay forever."

Jon paused in the act of filling her glass from a carafe of blush wine he had ordered. Then he nodded, seemingly pleased with her assessment. "It's always affected me that way. I'm glad it pleases you, too."

She took a sip of the fruity wine, let it tickle her palate and wander at will over her tongue before swallowing it. Already she could feel herself winding down, tuning in to the subtle textures that were all around them. "Before I knew where we were going, I told myself it really didn't matter, that being together was the main thing." She looked at him, a dreamy smile softening her face. "I was wrong. No other place could be this perfect."

He leaned across the table to clasp her hand, meshing their fingers. "If I have my way, this is only the beginning."

Cassy's heart drummed excitedly, certain that Jon wasn't referring only to the trip, but to his hopes for a long-term future, as well. It was what she'd been waiting to hear. The waitress interrupted her joyous reverie and, in a breathless voice, Cassy chose a Bavarian platter.

"This place has a European feel to it," she mused after Jon had selected cold seafood. "Sort of like—"

"A *gasthaus* in Bavaria," he finished. "I figured you'd noticed that because of what you ordered."

She laughed and confessed, "It looked like the biggest thing on the lunch menu. Being happy makes me even hungrier than usual."

"I'll have to remember that." Jon lifted his glass and took a very deliberate swallow. "If I can keep you happy and well fed, who knows where this might lead?"

Cassy's stomach did a back flip, and she clutched her glass like a lifeline. For the second time in only minutes, Jon had alluded to the future. This trip was already having an extraordinary effect on him, and it had barely begun. She touched his glass with hers, the sound ringing clear like a promise.

During the meal Jon told her about all the sights he wanted to show her and, in spite of the undercurrent of suppressed excitement, she managed to sound eager to play tourist. But she was even more interested in exploring what was going on between them.

"I glanced at the brochure in my room. It says there's a sauna next to the clubhouse. Want to give it a try after we finish here?

Jon speared his last boiled shrimp, bit it in half and chewed, all the while looking at her. "The one thing I don't need is something to make me hotter."

Cassy could believe that. She was experiencing meltdown by simply watching his mouth, knowing what delicious magic it worked. Wanting him had never been quite so imperative. "Then I guess you don't want to try the hot tub, either?" She was surprised she could speak at all.

He grinned, and it reminded her of a buccaneer ready to make off with the treasure. "Later, maybe. When it's dark. And everyone except us is asleep. Then we won't have to worry about . . . modesty."

She was sure the same vision was unfolding inside both their heads. "Uh, a nap?"

The grin became a laugh, wicked and promising. "Now that might not be a bad idea." His gaze moved from her parted lips to her breasts. "Sleep is way down my list of priorities for tonight."

CASSY TRIED TO REST but was too hyper to settle down. Instead, she had a long, bubbly soak, styled her hair in a cloud of soft curls and fussed with makeup, things she usually didn't take time to do. Tonight was different. Jon was taking her to dinner at the elegant Château Lake Louise, and he'd said, "Wear your best."

Now she was glad Meri had talked her into the rather extravagant shopping trip. Her purple Jacquard two-piece dress was relatively demure. The wrap bodice didn't show even a hint of cleavage, but the peplum had flirty little gathers in back that shifted with every movement of her hips. Of course, there was no denying the allure of silk and how it felt against skin. For later, she had another silk that was even more alluring....

The course of their evening was set when Cassy opened her door to greet Jon and saw the appreciative gleam in his eyes. "Trying to knock my socks off?"

"Mmm," she murmured with a discreet arch of her brows. "Is that possible?"

"More than possible," he said. "In fact, if we don't get out of here in a hurry, my socks and everything else will be off."

She gave him a look that said, "I can't wait," and went to get her jacket.

Later, seated in the formal intimacy of the Château, she was glad Jon had insisted on coming here. Cassy felt aglow in the flickering golden light. Jon had never looked so handsome. Nor, if her eyes weren't deceiving her, did he find anything on the menu half as delectable as she. Tonight fantasy and reality merged to create a perfect interlude.

"Eating by candlelight always makes me feel like a different person. I wonder why that is?" she said.

"Probably because it makes beautiful women even more so. And blunts the harsh edges of their men. Like champagne, it's a mood enhancer." Jon nodded once at the bottle their waiter extended for his approval. Within seconds the cork came out, its sound muted and nonintrusive.

Chateaubriand for two appealed to her, because it seemed to be an entrée made for lovers. But for one of the few times in her life, Cassy was too preoccupied to savor the meal. All her attention focused on Jon.

After dinner, they danced to slow, romantic music that demanded contact and conjured up visions of even greater intimacy. Being close, swaying in harmony, whispering their pleasure was a sweet, enticing substitute for the dessert they never got around to ordering.

She couldn't believe it was so late when the combo stopped playing and Jon asked, "Ready, Cassy? It's after midnight." She nodded, and in minutes they were driving away from the famous hotel.

Mellow from the atmosphere and Jon's attentiveness, Cassy lounged back in the corner formed by her seat and the car door. In the dash lights' reflective green, she studied his profile. She was sure any woman would find him marvelous to look at. But to her, his appeal went beyond physical attractiveness. He was a mature, serious man who approached life thoughtfully, and his decisions reflected that. He was also self-made and fiercely independent, a bonus in Cassy's opinion. She'd learned the hard way that not all men were so scrupulous about paying their own way.

She closed her eyes and smiled. Fate had been kind, sending her to buy a bachelor. "Do you remember that night at the auction?"

He chuckled. "How could I forget? For a while I was afraid I might collapse from a stress-induced coronary."

"I knew you were suffering, but it was something else that really sparked my interest."

There was a moment's hesitation, almost as if he were suspicious of the course the conversation was taking. "What else?"

"Your eyes. They looked intelligent. I saw that they sparkled even though I couldn't make out the color."

"I wasn't able to see three feet beyond my nose. You must have had a front-row seat."

"Nope, I borrowed Meri's opera glasses. Until then, I'd only previewed you from a distance. I didn't fully appreciate just how yummy you were."

"Uh, thanks, I think." It hadn't taken long to leave the small village of Lake Louise behind. Now they were on the main highway and surrounded by darkness. Jon easily negotiated the hills and curves.

"Then the mistress of ceremonies told us your eyes were green and full of naughty promises."

"She was full of—"

"Uh-uh," Cassy scolded. "She was right. Your eyes are very... expressive. They signal what you're thinking." She snuggled down in the seat, wishing she could read his thoughts now. Would they be as vivid as hers? "Know what else I could see through those binoculars?"

He readjusted his hold on the wheel. "No, what?"

"You might have changed your shirt and checked your socks, but you didn't shave." The car's forward motion faltered, then picked up again. "There was a shadow on your cheeks and jaw and neck. I wondered about... lower."

He made a sound but didn't speak.

"I liked the hint of beard. Very manly. Virile. I wondered how it would feel if you rubbed it all over me."

They speeded up measurably. "Cassy, you—"

"When you turned around to walk back to the microphone for the bidding, all I could think was how nicely your suit pants fit, and I was glad you weren't wearing the jacket. I told myself you'd taken it off just for me."

He cleared his throat. "I was hot."

Under his breath he added something Cassy couldn't make out, but she hoped it was a commentary on his present condition. "I think you got that announcer hot, too. She sure was eager to run her hands over you. But who am I to criticize? I wanted to do the same thing."

"Cassy," he said, and she could have sworn his teeth were gritted, "do you always talk to men like this?"

She smiled, though her voice was serious. "Nope. I've never tried it before tonight. But you're different, Jon. I'd never be so daring if I didn't know this is right."

"More like inevitable, you mean. I think it transcended 'right' weeks ago."

All during the ride, Cassy's heartbeat had been gradually quickening. It suddenly turned thunderous as the car raced even faster. "Does this mean you don't have any more reservations? That you're going to stop fighting?"

His head snapped around sharply before he looked back at the road. "Is that how you saw it? Me fighting you?"

"Going to deny that you resisted becoming involved with me?"

"Only at first, and only on principle. As soon as we met, things changed." He slowed to take the lodge road. "I wasn't exactly fighting, Cassy. Just trying to keep us from rushing a very big step for any man and woman."

"And now?"

"Now? Honey, I'm in a big rush."

7

CASSY WATCHED JON walk around the front of the car to open her door. He might have decided he was in a rush, but he couldn't do anything about it immediately. Though he'd bypassed the guest parking lot in favor of a closer one provided for day visitors, they still had to cross the bridge and walk around to their isolated point.

Halfway across the wooden span, Jon stopped and pulled Cassy to him. "I need a little something to tide me over." His kiss was slow, boundless and intoxicating, weakening her as only the touch of his mouth could. She was torn between wishing he had waited until they were in their cottage and wanting him to go right on kissing her.

With a heavy sigh, he released her lips and brought her head to his shoulder. "Your hair has been driving me crazy all night. I sat across the table from you and held you on the dance floor, all the time wanting to feel it curling around my fingers."

When he tunneled beneath the silky curls to lightly massage her scalp, Cassy's head moved sinuously, in time with the motion. "I'm glad you noticed. I wanted to look glamorous for you."

"You wanted to seduce me."

She snuggled closer, bumping his hips once gently, then again. "I'd say it worked."

"As you knew it would. That has never been in doubt. I think I was lost the first instant you looked at me." He draped his arm around her shoulders, and they resumed walking.

A small laugh escaped Cassy's lips. "I was afraid a stroll in this night air might cool you off."

"Even if that were the case, you could take care of it in about five seconds."

She tapped into the tightly wound anticipation in every movement of his body. It bound them like an invisible force. They reached their cottage and climbed the stairs to the second floor, and Jon took Cassy's key to unlock her door. Once inside she slipped off her quilted silk jacket and hung it in the coat closet. Jon followed suit, his gray pinstripe looking conservative next to the colorful Oriental pattern of hers. They exchanged anxious glances, and Cassy wondered if Jon had been struck by the same thought as she. Hanging up clothing side by side after an evening out was very domestic. Very married. Reminding herself that they were a long way from wedded bliss, she led him into the living area of her suite. "Would you like something to drink?"

"No."

"Anything?"

"Nothing. Thank you."

"You're welcome."

They laughed at the same time. She watched Jon debate, then sit on the raised fieldstone hearth. Cassy sank down onto a rattan love seat facing the fireplace and eased off her high heels, crossing her ankles on the wicker trunk. "In my fantasies I don't recall this awkward transition."

"I know," he said, examining the carefully arranged logs. "In mine, we're already pretty far along when I tune in. By that time, it's impossible to be inept in your eyes. You want me too much."

Cassy kneaded her arms. "I do want you. But for me there's no such thing as 'too much.'"

Anxiety shadowed his eyes, made his face tense. "I'm breaking one of my cardinal rules. Much as I want you, I can't help thinking it's too soon. I don't know enough about you, don't know what you expect of me."

She longed to give him a hug and say that she understood this was his last-ditch stand. She stayed put because she sensed that he needed to get it off his chest.

He got to his feet and stood behind a chair, facing her. "I've told you before, I'm not very good at being casual. Never had a one night stand or even a brief affair. To me sexual involvement is synonymous with long-term relationships. That's just the way I am, and I won't apologize for it."

"If you're bringing up those character traits to discourage me, it's the wrong approach. What you're saying sounds admirable. Any woman would be ecstatic to hear that from the man she's about to make love with."

He looked more dismayed than reassured. "I'm trying to tell you that I believe in loyalty and fidelity and...commitment. You need to understand that about me. And I—"

"Have my promise that I believe in the same things. We're not so far apart as you imagine, Jonathan. I trust my feelings. If you'll just let go and trust yours, a lot of the questions will be answered."

His hands tightened on the chair back. "My feelings have been in a jumble since C. C. Laurens paid ten thousand dollars for me, then coolly announced she had no intention of going on my Dream Date." With a sudden burst of aggressiveness, he stalked over to stand before her, arms crossed belligerently over his chest. "Well, Ms Laurens, do you think you got your money's worth?"

She could have shouted "Yes!" and meant it. Instead, Cassy let her gaze slide slowly from his dark brown hair to the tips of his Italian loafers, then back up. She challenged his defiance with a teasing wink. "Ask me in a couple of hours. By then I should have a better idea of your... worth."

"Dammit, Cassy!"

She was off the love seat in a flash, carrying through with the hug she'd wanted to offer earlier. "Jon, I've listened to your honorable speech and it was very impressive. But I think we've done enough talking."

She walked over to the fireplace, feigning interest in the stones. "Unless you're having second thoughts about wanting me."

"Hell, Cassy," he said, folding his arms around her from behind. "I want you so much I can hardly think about anything else."

Cassy closed her eyes as Jon nuzzled aside her hair and found the spot on her neck that was so susceptible to his mouth. His delicate nibbling sent flashes of heat racing to the core of her.

His hands moved with maddening languor along the curve of her waist, where they paused for only a heartbeat before beginning their climb. Cassy held her breath, willing him not to stop. To hurry. To end the torment by touching her *there*. When at last he shaped her breasts, lifting their aching weight with cupped palms, she heard herself whisper a plea for more.

He made a raspy sound and his lips moved on her neck. The words were indistinct, but the message was so clear her knees threatened to buckle. This was only the beginning of what he was going to give her.

The overlapping bodice of her dress allowed him easy access, and with daring curiosity he slid one hand inside. It glided restlessly over her satin-covered softness, while the other moved low on her stomach pressing her against him. Deep inside Cassy, the heat became a slow burn radiating out to engulf her. She abandoned herself to the feelings, wholly pleasurable and purely sensual.

Jon found and released the three concealed hooks that fastened her bodice and gently pushed the fabric off her shoulders. "Turn around, Cassy. Let me look at you."

Without hesitation she faced him. Hope and expectancy gleamed in Cassy's eyes as Jon touched the pulse thudding in the hollow of her throat. "You're as excited as I am," he said, but his gaze was fixed on the low-cut sweetheart neckline of her champagne-colored slip.

His thumb hooked under one of the gossamer straps and eased it aside. "I like what I see . . . a lot." He bent to brush her lips, and she felt the smile on his. "I'm about to show you how much."

"If the fire in your eyes is any indication, you're about to ravish me."

Jon sobered and inhaled sharply. "Close, Cassy. Damn close." He found the waistband of her skirt and freed the button. Purple silk billowed to the floor, and the searing heat of his hands branded her hips through the satin slip. She gripped his shoulders, swaying as the circular rotation of his palms on her derriere controlled her.

"Oh, Jon, let's not wait any longer," she whispered, burying her hands in his hair.

Agilely he shifted her into his arms and carried her the short distance to her dimly lit bedroom. He let her slide down the aroused length of him, then sat on the edge of the bed, keeping her between his legs, not relinquishing his hold on her hips. His mouth took turns at her nipples, dampening the satin, biting gently, drawing on them until they became tight and hard against his tongue. "I want to taste *you*, Cassy. Help me."

She complied, nudging the straps off her shoulders and down her arms with tremulous fingers. The thin layer of satin fluttered to her waist, leaving her exposed. Spellbound by the heated way Jon's eyes moved over her, her voice nearly deserted her. "I dreamed of you looking at me this way."

"Me, too. Endlessly," he said, his voice low and rough. "And about undressing you, touching you for as long as I wanted. Everywhere." He brought her close enough that his breath fanned the upper curve of her breasts. "Close your eyes, Cassy. Lean to me. Let me learn all your secrets."

As if by instinct, she did his bidding and was rewarded with the warm slide of tongue over nipples. The lush stroking continued, luring her with the shimmering promise of ecstasy.

"Ah, Cassy," he murmured against her dewy skin. He worked the slip lower, and it slithered down her legs, revealing her garter belt, stockings and minuscule briefs. Jon's gaze wandered with hungry possessiveness over what he'd uncovered. But he couldn't forego touching her for long.

She delighted in the intriguing contrast of his dark hands outlining the fragile bands of pale silk and lace and ribbon. Hands, she noticed with satisfaction, that weren't quite as steady or facile as they'd been only moments before.

Again Jon drew her breast into the moist warmth of his mouth, letting his tongue glide and circle and stroke. His index finger slowly traced a satin-ribboned garter down the front of her leg, along her stocking top and up her inner thigh. For just an instant his hand shaped her, but it was long enough to intensify the building heat.

Cassy felt weak, about to come apart at only the merest hint of what was in store for her. "Jon, my knees are shaking. I can't stand."

He rose quickly and lifted her onto the puffy comforter, stretching out beside her in the same action. "Sorry," he muttered, "I got carried away. You're playing hell with my control."

"Good," she murmured, "'Cause I have none left either."

Jon propped himself up on one elbow. His lips roamed feverishly along her neck. Then his tongue stole into her mouth, a delicious intruder bent on seduction. His slow, recurring pattern of advance and retreat drove Cassy to new heights of boldness. She took up his wanton cadence, matching his thrusts until they both were gasping. "Take it easy," he said, raising himself and kneeling astride her. "I haven't had time to do half of what I want to."

Languidly, and with reverence, he began to explore every centimeter of skin accessible to him. Her face, ears and neck came under gentle assault from the tips of his fingers. Her shoulders, breasts and midriff received the ardent attention of his mouth. Then he ventured lower and the heady temptation of release swirled all around her.

"My turn," she whispered when she couldn't take any more. She fumbled with his shirt buttons, nipping randomly as she bared his chest. "Let me do the same for you. I want to push you to the edge and take you over it with me." She reached for his belt.

"Don't, Cassy. I'm on a hair trigger, and it won't take much to set me off. I'm trying to do this right. It isn't easy." His splayed fingers spanned her stomach. "I want to make you feel things you've never felt before."

"You do. You will." Inside her the delicious pressure heightened and her hips undulated beneath his hand. She raised one knee and guided him to the snap holding her stocking up.

He concentrated on releasing the silk stockings and peeling them off her legs. A trail of airy kisses followed his slow, downward progress. "No one's ever been quite so dedicated to bewitching me."

She reached behind her, unhooked the garter belt and pushed it aside. "Are you bewitched?"

"Yeah, Cassy. Satisfied?"

"Close, Jonathan. Damn close." His insistent caresses were carrying her even further along the glittering path to fulfillment. "What I need now is all of you."

The Reluctant Bachelor

He stood beside the bed and stripped off his clothes, taking a fraction of the time he'd spent undressing her. Never once did his eyes leave hers. He approached her, a powerfully aroused, heart-stoppingly virile male.

But she read his slight hesitation as a sign of renewed doubts. He still clutched his slacks, as though he were contemplating escape. "Oh, Jon. Not now."

"Cassy..." he said, reaching into his pocket. "I can prevent you from getting pregnant. But I have to be honest. I'm not sure I can give you what you need in other ways."

She relaxed, knowing at once what he meant. He thought she needed promises for the future, promises he couldn't yet make. And, honorably, he was offering her one last chance to spare herself. Symbolically, she took the trousers from him and dropped them to the floor. "Jonathan, you don't need to protect me from pregnancy or anything else. I know what I'm doing, and I've taken care of everything. I know this is right." Confidently she skimmed the bikinis down, extended her hand and smiled. "Let me convince you, too."

This time he settled between her legs, and the part of him that she wanted most touched her tentatively. Cassy was jolted by the contact. She felt the potent affirmation of his masculinity, yearned for him to take her hard and fast. But he didn't plunge forward, didn't move at all. The cost of his restraint was evident in his savage grimace and the bulging muscles of his forearms that strained to hold him away from her.

"Please, Jon. Be inside me."

He looked beyond her eyes into her soul and began to enter her slowly—so slowly—until at last their bodies were locked together. He closed his eyes and was still.

Their shallow breathing was the only sound to breach the silence. He had claimed her. Completely. Forever. Cassy's fingers paused at his waist before straying to his flanks to hold him fast. "Jonathan, I can feel your heartbeat. Deep inside me, where we're joined. Can you feel mine?"

"God, yes," Jon moaned, forcing himself to not move. She was too tight, too sweet. Perfect. "Yes!"

But then he felt more. Cassy's body contracted around him as he drank in her primal sounds of demand and acceptance and surrender. Her eyes closed. She arched her head back into the pillow, lifted her hips and let the tremors he'd incited take her. Watching her accept from him the gift of pleasure moved Jon so profoundly that some guarded inner emotion broke free and sent him soaring. He thrust once, twice, again. Reality was suspended for a timeless interval. And when it shattered, he poured himself into her in a moment of consuming passion.

"Cassy."

All he'd done was whisper the name, but Jon felt as though he'd consigned his fate to her.

CUDDLED TOGETHER with their legs intertwined, Cassy revelled in the long mellow aftermath of shared satisfaction. At last she stretched luxuriously and smiled at Jon. "I have never felt as fabulous as I do at this moment."

When he didn't reply immediately, her elation faded. A little chill from nowhere zigzagged up her spine and replaced the lingering warmth. "Jon, if you regret being here, just keep it to yourself. At least for tonight."

He wrapped both arms tightly around her. "Regrets? Not a chance. I only meant—"

"If you're thinking it can get any better than what we just shared, then you must know something I don't. And if you do," she added, her voice a mild threat, "keep that to yourself, too. Let me assume I'm the best you've ever had."

"You are. That shouldn't come as a surprise." He rolled onto his back and pulled her over him. "You work powerful magic, Cassy. If you were any other woman, I wouldn't be here."

"So you've said. But are you sorry it happened?"

"Uh-uh," he said, embracing her for a long, deep kiss. By the time their lips reluctantly drew apart, Cassy felt him stirring beneath her thigh. "In fact, I'm thinking about doing it again."

"Thinking about it, huh?" Her audacious stroking helped him make up his mind very quickly.

"Ah, honey," he groaned, hips lifting off the bed, "I'm not thinking at all."

JON WOKE GROGGY and disoriented. His eyes refused to function, and he was in a strange bed. He was sprawled on his stomach with one hand hanging over the edge, his opposite foot trailing off the other side. He tried to clear his head by inhaling deeply. Faint traces of perfume and... loving. His eyes shot open.

"Cassy?" It was hardly dawn, but he could see her silhouette at the window, looking out over the lake. "What are you doing up so early?"

She glanced over her shoulder. "Habit. I tried to be quiet and not disturb you, in case you like to sleep late."

"Only on Sundays and vacations," he said, struggling to sit up. His vision had adjusted to the shadows, and what he saw blew any remaining cobwebs out of his brain. They were replaced by a now-familiar urge that hadn't plagued him so relentlessly before meeting Cassy. "Where did you get that nightgown?" Did his voice always sound so hoarse in the morning?

She came toward him, dressed in something straight out of a thirties movie. It was a lighter purple than the dress they'd left on the living room floor, and it conformed faithfully to every curve. "I'm glad you never got around to putting that on last night. I'd have disgraced myself for sure."

She twirled to display the gown's nonexistent back. It had a few straps, and the V slashed inches below her tiny waist. Everything critical was covered, but barely. Air whooshed out of his lungs. "God, Cassy," he said, reaching for her. "Did you know you've got a beauty mark right here?" His mouth touched the small brown dot at the base of her spine. "You're gonna drive me straight out of my mind." His tongue alternately circled and licked. "And I don't care."

She swiveled in his arms, and immediately he freed the small buttons attaching the straps to the front of her gown.

Her voice caught when she asked, "Didn't you say something about going to the top of one of the mountains today?"

"Later," he said, his words muffled as he directed his attention to more fascinating peaks. "We have all the time in the world."

A man of his word, Jon spent the next few hours leading her in a slow, steady ascent to oblivion.

8

"Guess I'm more of a sea-level-type person," Cassy declared between wheezes. She'd stopped for the umpteenth time to catch her breath. "Getting to the top of this mountain sounded like a piece of cake when that guy said the gondola would take us all the way up except for the last thousand feet. Talk about a snow job."

"Technically it's the truth. He just omitted saying that the remaining distance requires a forty-five-degree climb at seven thousand feet of altitude." Jon had halted several steps ahead of her.

"Your lungs must be more cooperative than mine. I feel like somebody put a giant rubber band around my chest." Her pace hadn't varied for the past fifteen minutes. Twenty steps forward—stop to pant—twenty more steps. It was humiliating. Especially with all those gray-haired couples passing her by.

"It's the altitude, Cassy," he offered solicitously as he walked back to her.

"You're just as high. Why aren't you breathing hard?"

He sent her a wicked grin. "Want to pop over there behind that boulder and see how long it'd take to get me breathing hard?"

Cassy laughed. One night had wrought a dramatic change in Jonathan. He acted more at ease than she had ever seen him, comfortable with their attraction at last. She hoped a week of being alone would be enough to start him thinking about how good they were with each other. How much better it could be if . . .

He was toying with her braid but looking into her eyes. "Feel like making the final assault?"

Cassy nodded. Squaring her shoulders purposefully, she took the lead. She wouldn't stop until she got to the summit. And she wouldn't give up until Jon saw that they belonged together permanently.

"Did it," she panted a few agonizing minutes later. "Hope the view is worth the climb." She made a complete turn, drinking in the majestic vistas from every perspective. "Oh, it is!" Cassy lifted her camera and captured shots of the serrated mountain peaks nearby and the distant snowcapped pinnacles that faded into gray at the horizon.

Satisfied that she'd taken enough photos, Cassy took Jon's hand, and they strolled out onto a deserted promontory. It was eerily silent except for the wind that buffeted them from all sides. They stood quietly for a while, savoring the magnificent setting. Finally she spoke. "Right now I feel as if this mountain belongs to us. As if you never shared it with another woman. And never will."

"Cassy—"

"No. You don't need to say anything. I know the difference between reality and fantasy. I've known for a long time. But while we're here, I'm choosing to suspend one of them."

He unlaced their fingers and turned her around to face him. "Cassy, this *is* reality." His fingers dug into her shoulders. "I've never come here with anyone else. Never wanted to." He seemed to be searching deep inside himself for something more.

"That's good enough for me." She suspected he was again feeling obligated to make promises because he thought she expected them. Or because in his mind, serious relationships deserved words of commitment. When he opened his mouth to speak, Cassy forestalled him with a kiss.

As always, desire was inherent when their lips joined. But today it was tempered with tenderness and a form of subliminal communication that hadn't existed before. There was another element present, too, one that was more elusive and conversely, more powerful. It loomed so significant that she struggled to give it a name.

When the word came to her, Cassy was swept up by a wave of euphoria. Love! From the beginning, she'd accepted that her relationship with Jon was inevitable, and by definition, love would be a part of it. But what she'd envisioned was mild compared to the feelings that swirled inside her now. Real love was vital and strong and consuming, almost tangible. She wanted to shout it from the mountaintop. She wanted to tell Jonathan.

Since she was reluctant to do either right now, she gave him another kiss, charging it with the full force of her newly discovered love, articulating that love without words. He responded so readily, so dynamically that Cassy believed his feelings were potentially as strong as her own.

"Wow," he said, swaying from the impact. "What did I do to deserve that?"

"I think I'll let you figure it out. Can't give away all my secrets, can I?"

"Tease," he accused, smiling.

For Cassy, love had elevated their kiss to a level beyond the physical. But when he pulled her hard against him, she realized it had inspired Jon in a much earthier way. His mouth hovered over her ear, his breath coming hot and fast. "I have a secret that I'll gladly give you."

"Is this a subtle way of telling me you're ready to go back to the lodge?"

"Subtle, hell, Cassy. I'm just plain ready."

LATER THAT AFTERNOON, Cassy crept silently out of Jon's bed and went across the hall to retrieve her camera. He'd fallen into a deep, exhausted sleep that would probably last for several hours. She'd have liked nothing better than to lie beside him, basking in the closeness and warmth. But another part of her wanted to steal away to the woods by herself and savor the past twenty-four hours. There was so much to reflect on, all of it exciting. She couldn't have asked for a more perfect rendezvous . . . or a more perfect lover.

The trouble was, she told herself as she struck out on the trail that circled the lake, she wanted more than a rendezvous, more than a lover. She wanted Jon to be in love with her, and say so. She wanted him to propose because he couldn't get along without her. She wanted to live with him for the rest of their lives. The only thing in doubt was whether and when he would decide he wanted that, too.

Jonathan had hinted that a week in paradise wasn't going to be enough for either of them. He had yet to clarify what that meant. Instead, he concentrated all his attention on making the most of their time alone. He'd visually and verbally seduced her during a long lunch, then took her to his room and pleasured her leisurely and well. But at the moment of climax, he had held her tightly and revealed a vulnerability she'd never suspected.

His whispered, "Don't leave me, Cassy," still echoed inside her head. Did he think she would? Or could? He hadn't made any secret that he didn't want her to go to Honduras. But his objections had always been based on practical factors. Today it had sounded as if the plea was torn from him in a moment of emotional defenselessness. It didn't seem likely that her going away for a while would inspire such an extreme reaction. And yet...

Maybe this morning on the mountain she should have confessed her love, reassured him that her trip did not diminish how she felt about him. The only reason she hadn't spoken of her feelings was that she didn't want to pressure him. Most people saw the admission of love as a demand for an answering vow. Cassy wanted Jon to say the words from his heart, not because he felt they were expected of him.

She left the path and picked her way to a small clearing on the lakeshore. A pine stump provided an ideal spot to sit and contemplate. She guessed she'd always assumed she would get married someday. But choosing to spend six years with the Peace Corps had taken her out of circulation at the time most women were finding mates. After she returned, organizing the Honduras project had claimed most of her attention. She'd given it willingly because, before Jonathan, nothing had been more important. Now she had flashes of uncertainty. Though it made her feel guilty, there were times when she almost resented the demands made by her work. Because of it she'd have to be away from Jon, something he clearly didn't want.

Don't leave me, Cassy. A little niggle of dread settled in her stomach.

"But it's only for a short time," she reasoned, focusing her camera on their cottage across the water. "Nothing will stop me from coming back to you." When Jon's bedroom window appeared in the viewfinder, a familiar excitement gripped her. Why was she out here alone when late afternoon shadows brought with them a penetrating chill? Jonathan promised warmth and security. Why was she wasting even five minutes of their precious allotment of time when all too soon her obligations would separate them?

Twice as fast as she'd hiked over, Cassy fled back to the haven of a fragrant fire and hot cider. And Jon.

"WHAT A DELIGHTFUL SPOT for a picnic!" Cassy exclaimed, raising her camera again. She'd shot three rolls so far that day. But she couldn't restrain her enthusiasm when everywhere she looked was another scene that just had to be captured. "This may be the prettiest place we've seen all week. And the hike up wasn't even too taxing."

She watched Jon survey the small meadow, a delightfully secluded treasure tucked away atop a plateau. Snowcapped mountains formed a bowl around them, and below, where they'd parked, the blue-green lake sparkled in the midday sun. "Everywhere we go, you say it's the prettiest."

"Well, it is. At least at that moment. But this setting is alive. Listen to those waterfalls welcoming us." All around them gentle cascades bubbled over limestone and shale formations. "This has to be the best of all. No question."

"You should be here when the alpine flowers bloom. A solid mass of color as far as you can see. Maybe sometime you can come back earlier in the season."

"I'd like to," she said softly, wishing he'd used "they" when he spoke about returning. "I imagine it's lovely any time of year."

"Yes. Except in winter you have to do your hiking on snowshoes or cross-country skis. But that's kind of fun, too."

Together they arranged their blanket next to a tall larch tree and set out the lunch packed for them in the lodge's kitchen.

Because they'd been on the go since early that morning, Cassy was famished. She filled their plates with seafood salad, cheese muffins and fresh fruit.

Jon watched her dig in and smiled. "Sorry you got cheated out of breakfast this morning."

She shook her head and finished chewing. "It was worth eating cold rolls to catch that moose drinking at the water's edge right after dawn. I waited almost twenty-nine years to see my first moose and may never see another."

"If you come back here, you're likely to spot at least one."

That was the second time he'd mentioned her returning to the lodge. But he was bent over, occupied with uncorking a bottle of wine, so Cassy couldn't tell if he was testing the waters to see if she was receptive to coming back or only speaking in generalities.

She examined the golden liquid in the glass Jon passed her. "You know, this week has made me remember why people look forward to vacations. It's been so long since I've taken one, I forgot how refreshing it is to escape the routine." He gave her an odd look, one she'd seen often enough to recognize. "I know. You probably figured I dash off to Europe several times a year."

"No," he said, not taking time to consider his answer. "Now that I know you, I realize you're no jet-setter. But everybody needs to get completely away from work once in a while."

Cassy shrugged. "I suppose. Lately, though, every time I get away it's *because* of work."

"I know. And soon you'll be leaving for Honduras." His hand stilled in the act of polishing a fat red apple, and he bit into it with a vicious crunch.

"You make it sound like the other side of the moon."

"It may not be all that far. But you will be gone for more than a few days. Even you don't know exactly how long."

"That's right," she said evenly, staring at a jagged range of peaks in the distance. It was better than looking at Jon, knowing what he would say next.

"Cassy, I know we've talked about this before, but have you given any more thought to the risk you're taking by going to Central America?"

"Some," she admitted, hoping this conversation didn't spell ruin for their picnic. "Mainly because it seems to bother you. Otherwise, I wouldn't think twice about my safety." She did look at him then, because she wanted to impress the truth of her next words. "Jon, I promise, nothing is going to happen to me."

He tossed the half-eaten apple to a squirrel that was busy hoarding food for winter. "How can you promise such a thing?"

"I just know I'll be coming back." *To you*, she added silently.

"Couldn't you hold off until later? Go down after the whole project is running smoothly?" There was an unmistakable brittleness to his compromise suggestion.

Cassy drew up her knees and rested her chin on them. "What would be the point of that?"

He didn't reply right away, but when he did, the forcefulness of his words shocked her. "I need you with me. I don't want you to go." As if recognizing that his admission cast a whole new light on their relationship, he added, "I mean, we haven't had much time together. Not like other couples trying to . . . It just seems to me that after this week, we ought to give ourselves a chance at a more, uh, conventional courtship. Doesn't that make sense?"

Cassy smiled, not at his discomfiture but at the idea of them on the requisite round of dates. "I don't think we've done too badly with this nontraditional courtship. I can't think of anywhere else I'd rather be than right here."

"That's what I'm talking about," he said, pouncing on her opening. "If you don't go to Honduras, we can see each other every night. Well, almost every night. We can go away for weekends. Vacations. You'd like that, wouldn't you, Cassy?"

She wondered if he had any idea that he sounded like an excited little boy. "I'd like all that very much, Jonathan. And my being away doesn't rule out our doing any of those things." She surreptitiously crossed her fingers that Gabe's decision about assuming recruiting duties would come before long and would be the one she wanted to hear. "We can start as soon as I get back."

"You won't change your mind about going?"

She shook her head. "I can't, Jon. This project has been my life for over a year. Don't ask me to give it up." She reached for his hand. "And don't put a damper on the first real vacation I've had since graduating from college."

"It's really been that long?"

"Over seven years."

"Then I'm glad I was able to lure you away for a week."

It was so peaceful here, so beautiful, she wished life could always be this satisfying. "You've given me the best vacation of my life, Jonathan." But it wasn't the place; it was him. They could have gone anywhere or nowhere, and the result would have been the same.

"There isn't much I can give you, Cassy. I know that. Have known it from the beginning. I've nothing to offer that you can't buy, more of and better."

If the stiffness of his spine hadn't told its own tale, she'd have thought he was joking. "This sounds trite, but most of life's important things aren't for sale. At least not those I want." She reflected for a moment, not expecting this alarming turn in the conversation. "You're capable of everything I value. Integrity, faithfulness and respect. Friendship. Love."

When he didn't look at her or say anything, she wished she'd kept quiet instead of pushing. "I only meant you have those qualities, not that I expect you to offer them to me. Stop fretting over what you aren't saying."

After that he did look at her, penetratingly. "I hate deception, Cassy. I don't ever want to be guilty of that where you're concerned."

"I've known where you stood every step of the way, Jon. You made sure of that. I've tried to make it equally clear that I'm willing to let things develop at a pace you're comfortable with."

He thrust her hand away and his eyes closed over what could only be described as pain. But when they opened again, they were alive with defiance. Within the span of a blink, she'd received conflicting messages. "You expect me to believe that? To think you'll be satisfied what whatever I give you?"

She met his gaze, nodded, knowing he wasn't finished and knowing she wouldn't like what came next.

"Then you're a naive little girl."

His accusation hit her like a sucker punch. What was he trying to prove? After all they'd shared, comments like that were ominous.

"If I was ever a naive little girl," she said, making a conscious effort to keep the hurt out of her voice, "I got over it ten years ago." Cassy felt him tense and reach for her hand. She let him take it, but for the first time, his touch failed to warm her. She wasn't particularly fond of revealing how gullible she'd been at eighteen, away from home for the first time. Yet she wanted Jon to understand that she'd learned the hard way not to trust every man she met.

She began haltingly. "I never thought of myself as sheltered, though I guess in a way I was. We always lived in the same place, knew the same people. Most of the kids I started kindergarten with graduated high school with me. I was always surrounded by relatives and friends. Didn't see myself or how we lived as anything out of the ordinary."

"But you were—are—a Laurens. Obviously you associated only with people like yourself. By definition, that is different from the rest of us."

Cassy had never had to contend with prejudice *against* her money. Usually it was the opposite. "Because of how rich you assume we are?"

"Naturally."

"It doesn't make as much difference as you might think, at least in my case."

He squinted into the sun, toward the highest mountain. "Dollars is dollars."

"So it would seem. The guy who set his sights on me when I was a freshman at William and Mary agreed wholeheartedly with you. He wanted an heiress—which one was secondary. Laurens just happened to be a recognizable name to him and, unfortunately, I was very trusting. I honestly didn't see it coming. I thought he was interested in *me*."

The meadow became even quieter than it had been. "What did he do?"

Cassy hesitated, then decided not to withhold anything. It wasn't the most pleasant of memories, but she'd written it off as a learning experience years earlier. "I suppose one's virginity is a small price to pay—"

"You mean the bastard—"

"You got it." Cassy gritted her teeth as his fingers nearly crushed hers. She tried to treat the incident as insignificant, something she'd become fairly adept at. It required her driest voice. "It's best to view the whole thing philosophically. It happens to most girls when they're in college, anyway. Why make a big deal out of it?"

Cassy could tell from the anger sizzling in his eyes that he didn't buy a word of her cavalier dismissal.

"Because, dammit, it is a big deal. And it shouldn't have been like that for you." When he spoke next, his grip had loosened and he'd controlled the turbulent expression. "What happened? You didn't marry the jerk, I hope."

A cloud scuttled in front of the sun, and Cassy shivered. "No, but if he hadn't tried to rush me into doing just that I might not have wised up until too late. Guess I'm lucky he got greedy and overplayed his hand."

Jon uttered a vile, one-word oath in an undertone. "Creeps who use women like that deserve to be strung up by the thumbs."

Cassy expelled a shaky breath. He looked capable of doing the deed himself. "I didn't tell you this to upset you. But you goaded me with that 'naive' remark, and I leaped to defend myself."

"I'm sorry, Cassy," he said, sliding closer so he could curve his hand around the back of her neck. "I'm still feeling my way. Sometimes I say stuff without thinking, and I know it hurts you." Self-disgust colored his words, and he rubbed his eyes. "Why am I screwing this up? It's like I'm trying to drive you away."

"You're just not sure what you want yet, Jon. But can't you try to accept that you don't have to reach a decision today? Or this week. Or next year. I'm not making any demands on you."

"That more or less confirms my point. I've always believed that a rich woman doesn't need a less wealthy man for anything." He stared straight ahead, his mouth grim. "Unless, of course, he possesses an incredible sexual aptitude that she can't find among her own kind."

Cassy jerked back, as though the bitter words had actually struck her. All along she'd supposed Jon's caution was innate. But his scornful denunciation was more than a casual observation. She had no doubt that some rich woman had worked him over good, and he wasn't about to forget the painful lesson. Cassy damned the heartless wretch—for making it so difficult to earn Jon's trust, but mostly for hurting him. She felt fiercely protective of the man she loved. Still, if he was willing to talk about it, that could be a first step.

"I guess if you want to get analytical, I don't need you *for* anything. I just need you. Period. And not because you possess an incredible sexual aptitude," she couldn't resist adding tartly. She was sure the remark hadn't been directed at her personally, but it stung, nevertheless.

"Jon, I'm sorry about whatever happened to make you feel that way. I think any woman who'd do something so destructive to you is crazy. Still, we all suffer disappointments in relationships. It's not fair to judge me, punish me because someone you cared about hurt you."

He looked at her as if she had started speaking in tongues, and she saw the denial coming.

"I don't know where you got that idea. Nothing could be further from the truth. How did we get started on such a pointless subject?" He yawned, stretched out on the blanket and put his head in her lap. She knew the laziness was a ploy to end the conversation. "We only have a couple more days. Let's not waste them. Come here," he said huskily, pulling her mouth down to his. "You haven't kissed me in at least an hour."

"That long, huh?" Cassy teased, her lips hovering just above his. Until Jon came to terms with his feelings, she'd be content to express her love in every way possible. "In that case, handsome, brace yourself. I've got a lot of catching up to do."

9

JON'S LIPS PLAYED with hers, first coaxing, then hungry, now tantalizing. How could each kiss be more meaningful, more satisfying than the last? Cassy asked herself. Love made the difference, she decided, drifting on a misty kind of awareness as his tongue again turned insatiable. Desire sparked fire and frenzy—exciting, but transitory. Love brought wonder and completeness, claiming a space that she hadn't known was empty. At last she understood why poets and composers had glorified it for centuries.

Contentment flooded her, and she abandoned herself to the serenity it brought. There was no rush. No need to reach out and greedily grab love, as though it would vanish if not seized and tethered.

The kiss took on a new element, sweeter, yet more profound, until the taste of him had branded itself on her so thoroughly that she'd carry it with her always.

A long rasping breath shuddered from him. "Cassy, wherever we are, I want you. Every time we make love, it's better. But the next time, I need you even more. As if I'll never get enough of you. I don't understand how that's possible."

She could have told him, armed with her new perception of love. But for now all that mattered was strengthening the bond they'd already formed. "It's the same for me. I think I know what to expect, then I'm overwhelmed by the things you make me feel."

Using the tip of her little finger, Cassy dipped inside his lower lip, using the moisture to paint his mouth. "I haven't seen or heard another soul since we got here."

He murmured his agreement, too occupied with sucking on her flirtatious finger to talk.

His head moving in her lap kindled an ache, made her feel voluptuous. Sybaritic. "We have this spectacular setting all to ourselves," she whispered.

"Mmm."

Jon had her finger trapped between his teeth, bathing it in the erotic wash of his tongue. And that wasn't the only part of her turning warm and wet. Cassy leaned her head against the tree trunk and angled her face upward. She was bold enough to initiate a seduction, but her muscles felt drawn out to the point of weakness.

The sun beat down, heating the wine in her veins. She dampened her lips and looked at Jonathan through half-closed lids. "I wonder what it feels like to make love in a mountain meadow, with nothing but sun and the scent of evergreen and each other all around you?"

"I don't know. But I'm imagining it. Right now." His voice was strained, and so were his jeans. He bent one knee and shifted his hips.

"Would you think me scandalous if I want to feel the sun on every part of me?"

He looked stunned for a second, then a slow smile spread. His gaze dropped from her face to her fingers working hurriedly at the buttons of her long-sleeved blouse. When she parted the edges to reveal her bare breasts, the smile faded and his lips went slack.

"Not scandalous," he said, making a choked sound of approval as his mouth feasted on her. "Delicious."

JON'S THUNDERING HEARTBEAT jarred him awake. He couldn't remember having a nightmare, but what else would leave him drenched and filled with something that felt suspiciously like terror? Cassy stirred, and a sick sensation slammed into him as it came back. This was their last morning at the lodge. The last time to wake tangled together, the same way they'd gone to sleep after making love.

He supposed they could steal an occasional night in Houston, but it wouldn't be the same. Nothing would ever be the same once they left Canada. How could he settle for a small part of Cassy when he knew what it meant to have all of her? It had only been seven days, yet he couldn't recall another week in his life that had affected him on so many levels.

Cassy had been a perfect companion. She loved the outdoors as much as he did, eagerly accompanying him on hikes, horseback rides and canoe trips, her camera snapping away as she got in "one more shot." There were afternoons when they had done nothing more than laze on the sun-washed deck with a book and melting looks that usually brought on "nap attacks," their euphemism for long, satisfying hours spent in each other's arms. The nights when they dressed up and went out, she became every man's ideal of a witty, sophisticated conversationalist. She made him laugh, made him think. And want. Jon had never wanted so much, so often, so obsessively.

And still, it wasn't enough. He needed more. If asked, he couldn't have said exactly what the *more* was. He just knew it existed.

He hadn't guessed that a week in utopia could completely blur reality and make a man daydream about things he'd never imagined wanting. But none of that mattered now. By evening, they would be home and Cassy would gear up to go her own way. Once again he'd be on the periphery of her life. He wasn't sure how he was going to handle that. His arm tightened around her, a reflexive defense against having her taken from him. He eased the pressure at once, fearing it might interrupt her sleep. Too late.

Eyes lambent, lips curved into a fanciful little smile, she always looked so good to him in the morning. He'd grown used to her, wanted her to be the first thing he saw every day. Cassy lightly clasped his shoulders, looked him squarely in the eyes and in a soft, sleepy voice said, "I love you, Jonathan Manning."

Love! The word made him reel. It took a moment to instruct himself to wipe the stricken, guilty look off his face. He felt as if he were playing hopscotch in a mine field. One wrong word, a careless gesture, and Cassy would be hurt. At all costs, he couldn't do that. He started to speak, but his brain didn't obey the command and supply him with the proper words.

If she had told him in the heat of passion, perhaps he could discount it. But he knew Cassy well enough by now to be sure she didn't make impetuous declarations. She said what she meant. Besides, he didn't want to refute her love. He found himself wanting, needing it more urgently than he'd ever wanted her body. If only...

"Don't worry," she said, soothing away the furrows in his forehead. "This isn't where you're expected to make a reciprocal vow of love. I've been telling you that all week." When he tried to protest, she sealed his lips with a light touch of her fingers. "I just wanted you to know before we go home. Somewhere down the line it might make a difference."

"It makes a difference now, Cassy. But I can't—"

"I know. You're not ready. I don't need the words."

She smiled at him so sweetly—so *lovingly*—that Jon's throat hurt. She was ripping him apart with her gentle understanding. Didn't she know how special, how precious she was? Cassy deserved so much more than he was giving her. He ought to be telling her he loved her, because he was sure he did. She was like no other woman he'd known, and the intensity of his feelings eclipsed anything he'd experienced in the past. Yet some churning inner fear prevented him from saying the words she claimed not to need. He didn't dare trust a love that had flared into existence so fast. It was impossible to trust that it could endure. But with time... He swore silently. His time was running out.

"It's our last day here, Jon," she murmured, fitting herself against him in the way he liked best. "Do you really want to go back to the mineral baths, or can I induce you to substitute some indoor recreation?"

Jon gave up. He couldn't think—about anything— with her hands slithering over him like that. "Induce, seduce, whatever you want. I'm yours."

ON THE MONDAY AFTER THEIR RETURN, Cassy was on her way out when two delivery people appeared at her door. Between them they carried a giant potted plant laden with yellow blossoms. "C. C. Laurens?" the female half of the team read from the small envelope bow-tied to a branch.

Cassy nodded, certain there must be some mistake. No one ever sent her flowers. Absently she directed them to place the plant in front of the French doors in the dining room, remembering a tip at the last minute. She was thinking ahead to reading the card tucked inside that envelope. As soon as she closed the door behind them, she hurried back to the dining room. The sweet-smelling scent had already permeated her apartment.

Her heart did a joyous dance when she took out the card and read, "You were—are—the best, Cassy. And so was last week." He'd signed it, "Yours, Jon."

She had cautioned herself not to expect romantic gestures from Jon. Yet there was no other way to interpret a riotously blooming plumeria and the tropical perfume it exuded. The scent invoked images of torrid tropical nights and everything that went along with them.

Cassy smiled and bent to smell one of the waxy yellow blossoms. Jonathan was turning out to be far more romantic than she'd given him credit for. That made her feel indescribably happy and filled her with hope. He hadn't given her the words yet, but if they could be together more, she was sure it was only a matter of time until he acknowledged that what he felt for her was love. Unfortunately she didn't have that luxury.

On their return flight yesterday, Jon had wanted to know what her week's schedule looked like. She'd dug out the notebook that she had purposely ignored while they were away and rattled off the list. He was disappointed that she would be leaving for Washington, D.C., late this afternoon and not returning until Thursday. But he had asked where she would be staying, then made a date for the night she got back.

She intended to shop for something special and have it delivered to Jon's office before she left. Cassy wanted him to know that he and their trip had been the "best" for her, too. She wasn't familiar with all the nuances of courtship, but what she'd learned so far was exciting.

"I MISS YOU."

Cassy sank onto the white-ruffled coverlet of her friend's elegant four-poster guest bed and yearned for a remote lodge in Canada. "Oh, Jon, I know. It's worse than before, isn't it?"

"Unfortunately, yes." Long-distance lines amplified his sigh. "Your meetings go okay today?"

"Everything's in good shape from this end." *Except that I'm miserable without you.* "I went out to dinner with some Peace Corps friends who now work in administration."

"It's always fun to get together with people you haven't seen in a while."

His observation sounded sincere, so far as it went. She wanted him to say the rest. "But?"

"I'd rather you get together with me. It feels like a year since I last saw you."

She had left Houston only yesterday, and they'd talked last night. Which made no difference at all. Every hour was agony when she wanted to be with Jon as much as she did. "Only one more after tonight, and then I'll be home."

The Reluctant Bachelor

There was a moment's silence, and Cassy knew what was preying on both their minds, even if neither would mention it. If four days' separation caused this much agony, how were they going to survive her weeks in Honduras? "I'll pick you up about seven, and we'll go out to dinner."

"I'll be waiting."

It was Jonathan who was waiting when she got back Thursday—on her doorstep. As reunions went, theirs was like a scene straight from the pages of the steamiest romance novel. Food was forgotten the minute the door closed behind them. They were too busy appeasing their appetites with each other. Finally, at midnight, Jon ordered pizza, and after they'd devoured every bite of the spicy, gooey indulgence, he offered to stay over. To protect her from nightmares caused by eating pizza so late, he said.

Any excuse sounded good to Cassy, but since he allowed her very little sleep, the problem didn't arise.

"WHAT AN EVENING," Cassy said with a sigh as Jon parked in the lot behind her fourplex. She'd wanted a replay of last night, but it had been Jon who'd insisted they accept Meri's invitation to one of her drama class productions.

"Care to take me inside and explain what that play was all about?"

Cassy laughed. "I'd like nothing better." They had so little time left before she went away. She intended to make every second count. As soon as they reached her apartment, she kicked off her shoes.

The Reluctant Bachelor 159

Jon did the same. Then he drew her into his arms and kissed her. "Can the discussion wait?" he asked with a sexy grin.

"Indefinitely." She tucked her fingers in his waistband and towed him toward her bedroom. At the door she turned, unable to resist another kiss.

She had just begun attacking his belt buckle when a deep male voice came from the bed. "It's about time you got here."

Cassy whirled around. "Alex!"

It was bad enough, Jon thought, to find a man in Cassy's bed. Worse still that the guy was good-looking in that scruffy, don't-give-a-damn way that women invariably found so appealing. Worst of all was watching Cassy fling herself onto the bed with him. He'd never considered himself a violent person. But seeing another man's arms holding his woman made Jon want to mop up the floor with him. Alex.

"Why didn't you tell me you were stopping off here?" she asked, giving the intruder yet another hug. "I thought you were going straight to Minnesota, and I'd see you there for the party."

Jon's ire rose another notch, and he felt his hands forming fists. Last night Cassy had mentioned having to fly to Minneapolis at the end of next week. She'd omitted that the purpose of the trip was to meet this man and go to a party.

"Uh, Cass, aren't you forgetting something?" Alex's gaze rested on Jon. "Looked like you were pretty interested in him a minute ago."

"Oh, yes," she said, scrambling off the bed. "Of course. Alex, this is Jonathan Manning. Jon, my unpredictable brother, Alexander. Fresh off the plane from Honduras."

Jon almost laughed in relief. The only thing stopping him was that Cassy's stone-faced brother didn't look as if he'd done much smiling lately. He looked about as murderous as Jon himself had felt moments ago.

"Come over here and tell me what your intentions are toward my little sister. Then I'll decide whether to shake your hand or flatten you."

"Hush, Alex," Cassy scolded, taking Jon's arm. "You're overdoing the protective big brother act. How come?"

"You can relax," Jon told a glowering Alex. "My intentions are honorable."

Alex sat up and the sheet fell to his waist. He looked at the bed—obviously aware of how it figured in Jon and Cassy's plans—then at Jon. "If honorable intentions mean you're going to marry her, I guess I should shake your hand."

"Shut up, Alex! In case you forgot, I'm a big girl. Jon doesn't owe you an explanation, and you're not getting one. Lay off!"

Cassy sounded angrier than Jon had ever heard her. In fact, he couldn't recall even once when she'd lost her temper. But now her braid was swaying and her gray eyes blazing as she tore into her brother. "Relax, honey," he said calmly. "This is your bedroom, after all. I'm sure Alex is only concerned that I'm not some... fortune hunter."

His strategy had the desired effect. Cassy laughed, exchanging knowing looks with Jon. "That joke's on you, big brother." She poked her toe through the pile of clothes beside the bed. It was clear that Alex had stripped to the skin. "Why don't we leave you to get dressed, and I'll make a pot of tea. Then we can talk."

For the first time, Alex looked away from Jon. He grinned at Cassy and dashed a hand over his bloodshot eyes. "Dilute it with about three fingers of brandy, and you've got a deal."

When they got to the kitchen and Cassy was filling the teakettle, she made a suggestion, knowing Jon would argue. "I think it would be better if you go home before Alex comes out." She switched on the gas burner. "I can talk to him and set him straight. He'll calm down when he doesn't have you to rant at."

"He isn't going to rant at me," Jon said, placing his hands lightly on her shoulders. "And I'm not ready to leave you yet. I don't want to leave you at all."

She turned into his embrace. "I'm sorry. I'm so tired of apologizing because something or somebody intrudes." She was glad to see Alex but resented that it cut into her time with Jon. "I had high hopes for tonight."

"Me, too," he said, his breath warm on her temple. "I want to be with you every night. It used to be that I couldn't sleep with anyone. Now I have trouble sleeping if you're not with me."

Cassy almost melted. He was so close to giving her the words that she could literally feel the love emanating from him. "Oh, Jon, I love you. Be patient tonight and let me talk to Alex. Tomorrow we'll go to your place. In fact, we'll turn off the phone and not surface for twenty-four hours."

"Sounds like the best offer I'm going to get tonight."

"I'll see that it's the best offer ever."

They both jumped when the teakettle announced its boil. It whistled like a freight train coming through the kitchen, heralding Alex's arrival.

Cassy's brother was tall and wiry and looked tough enough to handle himself and anyone else who wanted to take him on. A better ally than adversary, Jon decided as he set a mug and the brandy decanter in front of Alex.

Cassy filled their mugs and carried in a plate piled high with homemade peanut-butter cookies. "Why did you wind up in Houston?"

"Pretty much the same reason you settled here last year. It's the most manageable city with nonstop flights to Tegucigalpa." He tossed back a healthy shot of straight brandy and demolished a cookie in two bites, unfazed by the odd combination. "Had to make connections somewhere to get to Minneapolis and figured I might as well visit you while I was in town." He reached for another cookie, but his eyes were on Jon. "Looks like I got here just in time."

"I warned you, Alex. Don't start. That subject is not up for discussion."

Jon smiled when Cassy again rushed to his defense. But he could see a sibling showdown brewing. While he thought Alex was overreacting, he sympathized with the need to protect her. Jon didn't have a sister, but if he did and she was sleeping with a man, he'd want to make damned sure the guy wasn't just stringing her along. He understood that Alex was seeking the same sort of reassurance from him now.

"I care about Cassy." He could read the other man's thoughts as readily as his own. "I know what you're thinking. Her fortune has nothing to do with—"

The Reluctant Bachelor

"Hah!" Cassy interrupted, jumping to her feet. "What an understatement." Hands on her hips, she glared at her brother. "He has this thing about rich women. He can't stand them. Then I bought him at a bachelor auction." She switched her attention to Jon. "Tell him how you wanted to avoid meeting me simply because I had lots of money."

"She's right," Jon admitted, aware of how much he'd have missed by clinging to that misguided notion. "I was trying to think of a way to get out of our date."

"You must not have tried too hard."

"True," Jon said, calling on the patience he used in business negotiations. "Fate must have intervened to keep me from making the biggest mistake of my life."

Cassy's head snapped up; her eyes were wide with surprise. But Alex didn't give her a chance to speak. "You wouldn't be the first man to give my sister the rush while he was lusting after her inheritance."

"Alex," Cassy gasped. "You've no right to bring that up. My God, that has nothing to do with Jonathan."

"She told me about that two-bit con artist back in Virginia," Jon said tightly, his fingers gripping the hot mug. "And while I'd like to get my hands on the rat, Cassy's right. It has no bearing on what's happening between us."

"Oh, yeah?" Alex planted his forearms on the table and leaned forward, his tone accusatory. "I'm supposed to believe that Cassy—penniless—would be as attractive to you as she is now?"

"Yeah." Jon assumed a similarly assertive pose. He didn't feel intimidated, as Alex obviously intended. Nor did he take the insinuation personally. "Given the choice, I think I'd *prefer* she be penniless instead of filthy rich." Ignoring the glare Cassy had transferred to him, he went on. "But since there wasn't a choice, I had to accept the fact that I'm involved with a woman who could probably buy and sell me many times over."

He met Alex's challenge with one of his own. "If I can swallow my pride and live with that, and if it doesn't bother Cassy, then I'd say the case is closed."

Cassy watched the verbal combatants regard each other across the expanse of oak. At last, Alex withdrew with a shrug. "Okay, case closed."

She hadn't realized she was holding her breath until surprise at Alex's retreat forced it out of her all at once. The two must have reached a truce via some mysterious communication network that was silent and exclusively male. Cassy couldn't explain her brother's capitulation any other way. He was notorious for getting in the last word.

"I'm *so* glad your sense of honor has been appeased," she said wryly. "I was afraid you might feel compelled to challenge Jon to a duel."

The merest lift of Alex's brow signaled that he didn't appreciate her irony. "Don't kid yourself, sister dear. I still mean to find out his intentions. Meanwhile," he said, exaggerating a stretch as he unfolded from the chair, "I've brought you something from Honduras."

"Don't pay him any attention," she told Jon when her brother had gone into the bedroom. "He's always relished a good confrontation."

"It's natural for him to be concerned about your welfare, Cassy. So am I."

Because he spoke so quietly, sounded so wistful, Cassy was temporarily speechless. Before she could reply, Alex came back and took her hand.

"I happened to be up in your village a few weeks ago. Don Renaldo sent you this." He dropped a shiny silver coin into her palm.

Cassy stared at it for a long, heart-stopping moment. And then huge, fat tears started streaming down her cheeks.

10

MEMORIES CAME CRASHING headlong through the barrier of time and distance, transporting her back. So much to remember—small triumphs, wrenching losses, each in its own way building a legacy of hope.

"Cassy? Honey, what's wrong?" Jon scooted his chair closer to hers and laid a comforting hand on her shoulder.

She opened her mouth to reassure him, and all that escaped around the lump in her throat was a strangled sob. The surge of feelings gripped her, paralyzing her voice so that she couldn't speak. Cassy's reaction had been swift, powerful and purely emotional. It was also soul-deep and impossible to check. Her free hand groped for Jon, wishing it were possible to communicate her innermost yearnings by touch. She felt strength and warmth flowing from him as he linked their fingers, and she could almost believe he recognized the coin's real value.

Cassy's breath crested in choppy waves, only to break and build again as more memories swamped her. Blurred by a watery veil, she watched her fingers alternately open and close on the silver. At last her vision began to clear as the Kennedy half-dollar heated in her hand, radiating vitality and purpose and reaffirming her vision. At last, she closed her fist around it and clutched it to her heart. She would cling tightly to it always, because of what it symbolized.

Now she could speak, though her voice was halting and heavy with emotion. "I guess you both think I'm silly to cry over such a simple thing as a fifty-cent piece." Jon's grasp tightened, a silent warning that he wouldn't allow her outburst to be lightly dismissed.

She inhaled deeply and began again, this time to share an experience that, until now, she'd kept hidden like a well-guarded treasure. "The last night I spent with my host family in Honduras, I couldn't sleep, so I was lying outside in a hammock. It was very quiet and I was looking up through the trees at the stars. Don Renaldo, my host father," she explained to Jon, "came over and sat on the ground."

As if he sensed she was about to reveal something special, Alex claimed a chair across from them. "We talked for a long time, about everything imaginable—our little garden, what Peace Corps volunteers had meant to the village, nuclear war and what it would do to the world."

Cassy again studied the coin in her hand. "Then he started telling me about his six-year-old daughter, who'd died of fever before I came. Two years I'd lived with them, and they never mentioned that. As he talked, his eyes were bright with tears, his voice so full of pain he could barely get out the words. He said that what worried him most was fear of something similar taking his other children."

She dashed away an errant tear from her cheek. "I wanted so badly to assure him that his children would be safe, but how could I? He knew from experience not to expect such promises."

Jon smoothed her hair, as if he needed to offer some form of encouragement. "We sat there in silence for a long time, and finally Don Renaldo said, 'I would like to be able to give you something, Cassy. To repay you for what you have given my family and my village. But I have no money.'"

A shower of fresh tears plopped onto her and Jon's hands. "I couldn't help it. I started crying. Just like I am now. Because I had so much and I'd given so little, yet he wanted to pay me. Because I was leaving, and they had to stay behind. Because he didn't want any more than the chance for his children to grow up healthy."

Eyes still brimming, she looked at Jon, then Alex. "That doesn't seem like much to ask, does it?"

Her brother looked reflective, but didn't reply. Jon said only, "I understand," and for the first time, she thought that maybe he did.

"I THOUGHT ALEX might greet me with a shotgun when I came to pick you up," Jon joked. They had just finished an early dinner and had come back to his condo for the remainder of the weekend as Cassy had promised.

She rolled her eyes. "I think I finally got him off that track. We talked for another couple of hours after you left."

"About me?"

"Partly," Cassy admitted as she watched him unplug the phone and reach around the door to disconnect the one on the kitchen wall. She shivered a little, anticipating hours of delicious privacy. At her apartment too many people felt free to walk in unannounced or to call at any hour.

"What did you tell him about us?"

She glanced away from his incisive gaze, then met it with confidence. "The truth. That I'm in love with you."

"And?"

"And nothing. What else is there to say?"

His eyes narrowed and his features settled into a ferocious scowl. He went into the kitchen and returned with two slices of the cheesecake they'd brought from the restaurant. His expression was blank. "I don't imagine he did cartwheels when you made that announcement."

Cassy sampled a bite of the blueberry topping. "As you said last night, the subject is closed. And as I said, I'm a big girl. A twenty-nine-year-old woman doesn't need her brother's approval to have a lover."

"'Lover'!" he exploded. "Dammit, Cassy. Don't call me that!"

"Sorry." She set her plate on the marble coffee table. "I couldn't think of any other word." They both knew Jon was more than her lover, but he wasn't her fiancé. Since no in-between designation existed, a conversation headed in this direction was bound to get sticky. "Look, Jon, Alex is my brother and we work together. Neither gives him the right to meddle in my personal life. I simply won't tolerate it."

Jon smiled at the finger she was shaking at him. "Okay, simmer down. I just don't want him giving you a hard time because of me."

Cassy grinned and reclaimed her cheesecake. "Based on experience, I'd say it's an older brother's mission in life to give his kid sister a hard time. I learned how to handle Alex years ago."

"And still, he's willing to help you with your Honduran project. How involved is he?"

She watched Jon taste his cheesecake and make a face at its sweetness. He didn't share her love of desserts. "Well, he's not as obsessed with it as I am. Alex would be satisfied to study viruses and bacteria in solitary. But how could I not take advantage of a lucky break when he was sent down there to gather research data. As soon as he came on board, he really got things moving. The timetable might have been delayed for months without his efforts. He's done all the liaison work with Honduran government agencies setting everything up for our volunteers."

"You know, Cassy, what you said last night, about your host father and how he worries about his children's future... I've been thinking about it all day." He shifted on the couch, as if it were uncomfortable. "I've... well, I've never been much of a joiner. But if a contribution would help, I'd like to do that. How does ten thousand dollars sound?"

The amount was equal to what she'd paid for him at the bachelor auction. Cassy's pulse increased measurably. She felt as if she'd just been presented the crown jewels. Not because of the money he was pledging, but because it represented a show of support for her work. "Thank you," she said softly. "That's very generous. You'd be astounded to know how many children can be vaccinated for that."

Looking solemn, he reached across to take her hand. "I want to be involved in whatever is important to you, Cassy."

"You're the center of everything that's important to me, Jon. I don't want you to have any doubts about that."

TWENTY-FOUR HOURS hadn't sounded like much, Jon told himself as he drove to Cassy's apartment on Tuesday evening. Yet they'd made the most of them. They had talked—really talked—about what was meaningful in each of their lives, and also about silly escapades in their past. She'd shared a great deal about her family; he'd revealed a little about his. To be expected, he reasoned. She had a lot more relatives than he did.

Their lovemaking was less frantic, more natural, as if they had been with each other for years instead of weeks. Jon didn't know how it was possible that the ease was infinitely more satisfying than the hot desperation he'd felt at the beginning. It wasn't that his passion for her had abated, but rather that it had been tempered by the fires into something stronger and enduring. He couldn't envision a time when he wouldn't want to make love with Cassy. Still, it was only a part of the ties that bound him to her.

And she loved him. He couldn't describe how that touched him. He only knew that he wanted to hold on to the feeling forever, needed to keep hearing her tell him. Several times he'd been on the verge of saying the words, too. But they always backed up in his throat. Jon figured that until he could tell her with no effort, he'd keep quiet. Cassy deserved love without reservations. For the hundredth time, he asked himself why those three words were so difficult to say when everything else seemed so right.

Being with her was the key. Knowing that, he vowed to spend every minute Cassy could spare resolving his perplexing reluctance to commit himself fully. He disliked having to go out of town last night, but he couldn't avoid it. Tonight she was speaking to a fraternal organization in the NASA area. He'd taken off work early so they could grab a quick bite before he drove her down and sat in on the speech.

"How does Mexican sound?" Cassy asked when Jon came to pick her up. "There's a pretty good place not far from here. Kind of a dive, but the food is tasty."

He agreed to her choice, and she hauled out a man-size shoe box. When she began pawing through the contents, he asked, "What is all that mess?"

"Coupons. I know there's a two-for-one in here somewhere." She upended the box, fanning the slips of paper over the tabletop. "I hope it hasn't expired, but sometimes they don't pay attention to that."

Jon experienced a flash of annoyance. "Cassy, I can afford to pay for two dinners at a Mexican joint."

She glanced up briefly in reaction to his sharp tone. "That's not the point. Heck, I can afford it, too." She grinned impishly and held up the dog-eared coupon like a prize. "I know I'm eccentric about spending money, but indulge me, okay? Everybody's got their little quirks."

Several hours later they arrived at the hotel where Cassy was speaking. There were at least fifty men jammed inside the meeting room. Jon wondered how many of them were sincerely interested in medical care for a small Latin American country and how many were curious about Cassy.

She disarmed them by beginning, "Did you ever think you'd hear someone named Laurens begging for help and money?" Following the laughter, she elaborated. "At our house, we learned to do this early. For as long as I can remember, my family instilled public service as a duty and responsibility incumbent upon those who'd been born as fortunate as we had. I accepted that without question.

"So I joined the Peace Corps and was sent to Honduras." She clutched the podium and looked out over her audience. "Can any of you even imagine a nation where the population doubles every twenty years? One where more than eighty percent of its citizens suffer from malaria and malnutrition?" She cut immediately to a slide presentation, visual proof that she hadn't exaggerated.

"The second night in my Honduran village, I was lying awake because I hadn't yet become accustomed to sleeping in such austere surroundings. I heard a whoop. I figured it must have come out of some exotic animal—no human sound could be that chilling." She stepped away from the speaker's podium and came close to the edge of the raised platform, close enough to touch those in the first row.

"Within minutes, all I could hear was coughing and crying. In Spanish, it's called the 'the savage cough.' For the rest of my life, it will mean death. Senseless and avoidable."

The audience sat poised, and so did Jon. "For days, none of us slept. During the epidemic, we took time out for funeral marches. Tiny, brightly colored caskets borne along behind the guitar players and followed by weeping, devastated families."

Cassy didn't try to disguise the anguish in her voice. "You can't witness something like that and ever, *ever*, be the same."

Silence reigned as the crowd reflected on how Cassy's experience had affected her. It was clear that incidents like the one she'd just related were her motivating force.

Then, like a master hypnotist, she freed them from the trance. "Everywhere I've traveled, I have met so many generous people, busy like yourselves, yet willing to give up a week or two of their time and share their skills to help alleviate this and other tragic, self-perpetuating problems."

Once again she became accessible, appealing. "In about two weeks I'll be accompanying the first team of twenty volunteers to Honduras. With the help of caring individuals like those of you here, we hope to build a continually rotating pool of talent so that there will always be personnel there, carrying on the fight. I hope some of you will be inspired to join us."

Jon's ears buzzed, but he could hear distant applause. Two weeks. That was all the time he had until Cassy went to Honduras. He'd known all along she was going. Knew he didn't want her to. But hearing her personal recollections tonight and responding to the fervor along with the rest of those present, triggered a fear more real and immediate than what he'd felt up to this point. How could he hope to compete with such lofty idealism?

What a nasty trick fate had played. He had at last met the one woman he wanted to spend the rest of his life with, only to find her dedicated to a cause that consumed her more than love ever could.

He sat mute and unmoving for nearly an hour while she answered questions and accepted business cards from the men who were interested in helping her. Jon didn't trust himself to move, didn't know what he might do or say.

He felt like a man on the edge of madness. Surely only a selfish monster would want to prevent a humanitarian like Cassy from doing her vital work. But heaven help him, that's exactly what he wanted to do. He needed her, too. How did a man protect himself against such desperate need?

By the time she glad-handed her way back to Jon, Cassy knew something was dreadfully wrong. The organization's president was walking with her, so out of politeness she performed a hasty introduction. Jon mouthed the correct words, but she could see his eagerness to get out of there.

As the three of them walked to the parking lot, she thanked the president for allowing her to speak and promised a report after she returned from Honduras. When they were out of earshot, she asked Jon, "Are you ill?"

"No, Cassy, I'm fine." Mechanically, he opened the car door for her.

She waited for him to come around and get in the driver's seat. "Did I say something that upset you?"

"Your presentation was extremely moving. It got to me, just as it did to everyone else." Very deliberately he inserted the key into the ignition, stretching out the tension until she felt like screaming. "Oddly enough, all I can think about is you taking off in two weeks. Going to Honduras. Leaving me."

"I'm not leaving you! Where did you get such an idea?"

He shrugged and started the car, backing it out of the parking place. Every move seemed to require more strength than he possessed. Cassy couldn't accept that her leaving the country for a short time would hit him with such an impact. "We both knew this was coming—"

"I guess I thought I could stop you. I suppose I should have known better. Instead, I let myself get deluded into believing something when I knew it came out of nowhere too fast and too good to be real."

Under the cynicism she heard despair. "Jon, what are you talking about? You make it sound as if I'm going away forever."

"You will."

His quiet resignation made her panicky. "Just for a few weeks. I'll be back so fast you won't even miss me." Cassy doubted she could sway him with platitudes like that one.

"I miss you already."

The words were wooden, detached. He was withdrawing before her eyes. "Please, Jon. You sound so strange. You're frightening me."

"Am I? Then I guess I'd better not say anything else."

He didn't. Not during the rest of the interminable trip to her apartment. No matter what argument Cassy put forth, it was met with silence. She couldn't reach him at all. He had apparently tuned her out and was now listening only to some wrong-minded internal monologue. How could she change his mind when he refused to hear what she was saying?

The Reluctant Bachelor

When they pulled up in front of her building and Jon didn't even shut off the ignition, Cassy decided to take drastic action. She leaned across to plant a brash, unexpected kiss on his mouth. At the same time she shut off the engine and pocketed the keys.

"Why did you do that?"

"Saints be praised. He can still talk."

"Cassy, don't push it."

"I copped the keys so you'll have to come inside. Where, if you don't start listening to me, I may tie you up. But trust me, you're not going anywhere until you've given up the absurd idea that I'm leaving you."

He let out a sigh and followed her without the argument she had expected. In the living room, she urged him onto one end of the sofa while she sat at the opposite end. "Now, Jonathan, we both know how much you value logic. Right?"

He nodded, lapsing into the silent treatment again.

"Well, chew on this logic. I love you. Translated, that means you're stuck with me. Unless you kick me out, though I'd advise against trying that." The remote look in his eyes was gone, and Cassy took heart that his features were becoming more animated.

"Jon, I can promise you that even if we were apart for two *years* I'd still love you. It has nothing to do with logic or anything else we can control. I love you. Nothing is going to change that. Please try to remember that when I'm in Honduras."

He stood and began pacing, an action that didn't seem in character. "Cassy, I've said all along that we were rushing into this." He stopped and held up one hand. "I'm not heaping the blame on you—I realize I'm equally guilty. But maybe..."

The Reluctant Bachelor

Guilt? What did guilt have to do with anything? The room tilted slightly and took on an eerie cast. Cassy suddenly felt very warm, uncomfortably so. Odd. The past few nights had been so cool. And what was the matter with Jon? He was weaving around the room like a drunk, when he hadn't had a drop of anything alcoholic. What was going on?

Oh, no. Those vaccinations she'd had today. They did her in every time, simulating the absolute worst case of flu.

"What I'm trying to say is that . . ." Part of his words faded entirely while the rest ran together in a nonsensical blur. When she attempted to tell him, her voice came out as distorted as his.

"Jon, I'm so tired. Can we talk tomorrow?"

"Cassy, are you okay? You look flushed."

Jon was kneeling in front of the couch. She saw his lips moving but couldn't hear anything except the keening sound inside her head. No matter. She was too tired to answer, anyway. If she closed her eyes, she could rest and shut out those black blobs that were swimming in and out of focus.

"Cassy, look at me."

She could hear Jon's voice clearly now, but he sounded so frantic. He wanted her to open her eyes. She would gladly do as he asked, if only she wasn't so tired. Maybe if she could just lie down . . .

"Honey, tell me what's wrong. Please."

At last she summoned enough energy to raise her lids slightly. Jon's face loomed over her, creased with concern. "Wrong?"

"You look like you're going to pass out."

"Ridiculous. I don't know how to faint."

"I think you almost learned," he said with a shaky smile. "Cassy, are you in pain?"

She tried to struggle upright. It wasn't worth the effort. "Just tired. So tired and hot."

He touched her cheek. "Damn! You're burning up. Who's your doctor?"

"Not to worry." Her hand flopped like a flower with a broken stem, and her entire body ached as though a herd of elephants had stomped over it. "Just my shots. Make me sick every time."

"What kind of shots?"

Cassy didn't feel like chatting, but she could never refuse Jon anything. "Smallpox, typhoid, typhus, yellow fever, plague, cholera. A bunch more. Alex's fault. Said to get 'em."

"Not all at once, I hope."

All this talk was wearing her out. "Be fine tomorrow. You gotta go. I'll sleep here."

That was the last thing Cassy remembered until she opened her eyes to sunshine. And Jon. He was in a chair beside her bed. She'd bet he hadn't slept at all. "I hope I look better than you do," she said, feeling chipper enough to attempt a small joke.

"Nurses aren't supposed to look good. It gives patients ideas that are harmful to their health." He came over to check for signs of fever. Cassy touched him the same way. His beard felt as sandpapery as his voice sounded. "How do you feel?"

"Weak, hungry and in need of a bathroom. What time is it?"

"A little after noon." He pulled back the sheet and lifted her into his arms. "Carrying you to the bathroom," he answered before she had time to ask the question.

"I'm not an invalid," Cassy protested, unaccustomed to this kind of treatment. "I can walk."

"I'm sure you can. I'm just not letting you." He deposited her inside and walked back to the doorway. "Don't get any brainstorms about taking a shower yet. I'm going to put some food in you, and after that, we'll see."

"Who put you in charge here?" she demanded, though she was secretly pleased by Jon's solicitude. She dimly recalled telling him to go home, assuring him that she'd be all right. But he hadn't listened.

"I put me in charge. Later, maybe we'll see if you've got what it takes to overthrow me. In the meantime, resign yourself to following orders like a good soldier." With that he closed the door behind him.

Cassy knew she wasn't yet strong enough to defy Jon and attempt a shower, much as she'd like to. But she did manage a quick wash, brushed her teeth and sprayed on some cologne. By that time her legs felt rubbery enough that her bed looked like an oasis in the desert.

A while later, Jon carried in a tray and placed it on her lap. He'd raided the pantry for a can of corned beef hash. On top of that was a pair of perfectly poached eggs; on the side, some tomato slices and cheese-toast triangles. "Do you think you can eat this?"

She scooped some of the egg yolk onto her toast. "If the day ever comes that I can't eat, call the undertakers 'cause I'll be a goner."

"I was worried last night, Cassy," he said soberly. "You were so hot, and before I knew it, the bed was shaking from your chills."

The Reluctant Bachelor

She paused before taking a bite of hash. "I'd forgotten that those shots always hit me like a bad case of flu."

"I checked with my doctor, and he told me it affects some people that way. Said all I could do was keep you warm and quiet."

"I know. This has happened before. There was no reason for you to worry. Or to stay here, for that matter." She vaguely recalled her disjointed sentences and realized they probably hadn't made sense. "I tried to tell you I'd be okay."

"Do you really think I'd just walk away and leave you in that condition?" He sounded offended. "Caring about someone means being there when that person is sick and needs you. Wouldn't you do the same for me?"

"You know I would."

"Then I don't want to hear the phrase 'I can take care of myself.' I'll decide when you can, and until then, you're not getting rid of me."

For the rest of that day, Jon ordered her to stay in bed. He waited on her like a personal ladies' maid, bringing food, tea and juice and an endless parade of other things he thought she might want. Before dinner, when Cassy insisted on a shower, he argued that she wasn't strong enough. They finally compromised and he drew a bath, then drove her crazy coming to the door every thirty seconds to check if she was okay. He slept with her that night, holding her tenderly after he'd given her a back rub.

Jon's attentiveness was adorable, but Cassy wasn't used to anyone fussing over her. A little bit of that went a long way.

By the next morning she felt fine, if still a little shaky. "I think you should go back to work," she said as a prelude to bringing up her own activities. "Actually, you shouldn't have missed even one day." That had been a constant bone of contention, but Jon was unshakable.

"We'll talk about it tomorrow." He continued to brush her hair as she sat up in bed. "You do look a lot better. But one more day won't hurt."

"Uh, Jon, I have to go to Minnesota tomorrow afternoon."

"You've no business traveling," he said stubbornly. "You're still weak."

"Only because you won't let me do anything. If I can move around, I'll gain strength. Trust me, I know how this thing works." She picked at the sheet and waited for his reaction.

"We'll see." Hands in his pockets, he walked over to look out the window into her backyard. "I could go with you. Make sure you're all right."

Cassy did a double take. He wasn't looking at her, perhaps because he suspected she'd veto his suggestion. "That might not be a very good idea."

He swung around, challenging. "Why not? Ashamed to introduce me to the family?"

"That doesn't deserve an answer. Of course I'm not ashamed to introduce you." Indeed, she'd like nothing better. But she knew her family would attach great significance to his presence. "It's just that if you show up with me, Alex is likely to get the wrong idea. Blabbermouth that he is, he'd probably spread rumors that we'd have to deny."

His head was lowered, as if he were in deep thought, and he didn't reply.

"All I'm saying is that I don't usually bring male friends to family gatherings. If I show up with you,

The Reluctant Bachelor

everyone will make assumptions. Like most families, they're excessively preoccupied with the fact that none of us is married yet. You'd be the target of rampant speculation, and they're not above asking embarrassing questions."

He stalked back to the bed. "I can handle the questions. I'm not some wet-eared swain who'd wilt under pressure."

"Of course you're not. I just don't see any sense in your enduring that if you don't have to." Under the sheet she crossed her fingers. "There's no real reason for you to be there."

A muscle jumped in his cheek; she saw his hand working inside his pockets. "There's one very good reason, Cassy. To be with you. Now stop arguing and give me your flight numbers so I can call for a reservation."

"Check the notebook in my purse," she said, hearing the smile in her own voice. "And don't say I didn't warn you."

His grin wasn't that of a worried man. "Something tells me you're in for a big surprise, honey."

11

ONCE JON DECIDED to accompany her, Cassy had been able to convince him to go to his office and catch up on his work before leaving again. She had a lot of details to take care of and would never be able to get them all done with him there, fretting about her overexerting.

Much as she needed a breather from his hovering, she saw it as a positive sign of how much he cared for her. And she was ecstatic that she'd failed to discourage him from going with her to Minnesota. He dismissed her warnings so handily she wondered if maybe he *wanted* to meet her family. Another positive sign. After she'd confessed that the occasion was a joint celebration of her and her father's birthdays, he was even more convinced he'd made the right decision. If only the Laurenses' penchant for saying whatever came to mind didn't send him running in the opposite direction, it might turn out to be an interesting visit.

Cassy called her mother to report that Jon would be coming, too. She briefly considered asking Emily Laurens to warn everyone else not to pump Jon for information about himself or his "intentions," as Alex had phrased it. In the end she rejected that idea. Her parents might try to cooperate, but knowing her siblings, they'd do just the opposite out of sheer perversity.

Her next call could have more impact on their future than her and Jon attending a family reunion. When

The Reluctant Bachelor 185

she'd phoned Gabe last Saturday morning to wheedle a weekend invitation for Alex, she hadn't mentioned her request for his help. She didn't want to push her luck by asking for too much at once. This time when she called to thank him for "baby-sitting" her brother, Gabe actually raised the issue himself. He didn't say he'd sign on, but he did tell her that he was leaning heavily toward it. He just needed a while longer to be certain. Cassy understood it was essential that she not pressure him. She only hoped he decided soon.

At first she blamed superstition as the reason for not telling Jon about her plans for Gabe. Foolish as it was, she clung to the old adage that a wish divulged was a wish denied. Now she realized that what really stopped her was the dread that she might get his hopes up only to have Gabe disappoint them both. It would be so wonderful if she could give Jon the good news as a parting gift before going to Honduras. He might not be so disturbed by her leaving him this time if he knew it wouldn't be happening often from now on.

She'd been so tempted to reveal her secret after the NASA speech, when Jon had become so upset. For a time he'd sounded as if he wanted to retreat to an earlier, less intense stage of their relationship. But the second she started feeling ill, he turned protective and tender and thoughtful. Cassy had to believe those actions reflected his true feelings. His insistence on making the trip to Minnesota with her further reinforced that belief.

Jon gave every appearance of a man falling in love.

FRIDAY, WHEN THEY CLEARED the ramp that connected to the jet way, Cassy grabbed Jon's arm and drew him aside. She pointed to a man leaning against an iron railing. Dressed in wrinkled khaki pants and a plaid shirt, he had the bewildered look of someone who, while aware of where he was, couldn't quite recall what he was doing there.

"That's Poppy—my father. The vague-looking one," she added with an affectionate smile. "If we don't go remind him he's here to meet us, he's apt to take root over there."

Despite Cassy's description, Jon thought it unlikely that Edwin Laurens was slow-witted. She had told him her father headed the research and development arm of the family corporation. Leaving management in the hands of a younger brother, he spent the bulk of his time in the laboratory and was responsible for a number of significant advances in medical technology. "Your typical absentminded professor, huh?"

"You got it. Ten to one his head is full of heart valves or artificial joints or whatever project he's working on at the moment." She slipped her hand in his. "Let's go snap him out of his reverie."

She pecked him on the cheek, and Mr. Laurens blurted out, "Cassy, you're here," as if finding her at the airport startled him. Father and daughter exchanged hugs, then introductions were traded.

He shook Jon's hand, obviously trying to place him. "Your mother said you were bringing someone with you, but I don't recall her saying it was a young man. Figured it was that friend of yours, what's her name? The tall redhead who always gets Alex in such a snit." He laughed.

Jon did, too. "I can imagine that pair locking horns. Must be entertaining."

Edwin nodded. "I expect Alex will take to you better than he did to 'that Amazon,' as he calls her."

Jon didn't contradict the older man, but he couldn't picture Cassy's brother rolling out the red carpet for him, either. Last weekend they had effected a wary truce, mainly for Cassy's sake. Not that Jon didn't want to get along with Alex; he did. He wanted all the Laurenses to accept him. A novel situation, he thought with a smile. At one time seeking approval from a woman's family would have made him worry that he'd got himself in over his head. Now it felt right.

Since they were only here for several days, they had brought carryons. After Edwin consulted his parking ticket—Jon assumed he'd written down the precise location so he didn't lose his car—Cassy led them out to the covered ramp. Jon almost snickered when he spotted the rusty old station wagon. Its back bumper was crooked and the fake wood on the sides was faded and warped.

While her father tinkered with a stubborn lock, Jon commented to Cassy under his breath, "Devotion to clunkers must be hereditary."

With a deadpan expression, she said, "What do you mean? This is the good car. You should feel privileged that he borrowed Mother's."

About forty-five minutes later, when they halted alongside an even older sedan, Jon saw that Cassy hadn't exaggerated. Though she had repeatedly informed him that their life-style wasn't opulent, this was not what he'd expected. He guessed the property covered two to three acres, and it was on the shore of Lake Minnetonka, but it lacked the meticulous, landscaped layout of a typical estate. The brick house was old and large—they were a big family—though his builder's eye noticed that it could stand a good bit of maintenance.

From the garage they trooped through a cluttered mudroom and into the kitchen, where Cassy's mother was giving instructions over the phone. When she finished, Emily Laurens put one arm around her daughter and offered the opposite hand to Jon. "Good thing your plane wasn't late. There's so much to do."

Cassy patted Emily's hand. "There's always a lot to do, Mother. Do you suppose we could put our bags upstairs first?" After gaining a temporary reprieve, she and Jon climbed wide walnut steps to the second floor. "The secret to avoiding my mother's endless list of chores is to stay out of sight. It drives her crazy to think someone might be idle for even a second."

"Don't be too critical. You probably learned your organizational skills from her."

"You're right. And I've needed every one of them." Casting a pensive look toward her room, Cassy showed Jon into the guest suite that, along with the master, formed a separate wing. She checked the bed for sheets and pointed to a bath that was shared with a second guest room. On tiptoe, she brushed her lips over his. "I wish we could be together. It's—"

He cut off her words with a kiss that for all its gentleness was very thorough. "No problem. I'm here to fit in, not make waves. We don't have to flaunt anything."

"Thanks for understanding." She gave him another quick kiss and picked up her overnighter. "Guess I'd better drop this off, change and go down to get my assignment. Remember, just hang around up here or sneak out the front door. See you later."

By the time Cassy switched to jeans and went downstairs, Jon was in the kitchen, having exchanged his slacks and sport coat for sweatpants and running shoes. As predicted, Emily was giving him instructions.

"I had to send Ed back to Wayzata after the birthday cakes. He forgot them on the way home. Since Alex is using the aunts' car, he's running their errands before bringing them back for the cookout. Kevin," she said, shaking her head at the mention of Cassy's younger brother, "as usual, has managed to escape. I lost track of him, and first thing I knew, the sailboat was disappearing around the point. He's probably lost to us until he smells the food."

"And Meghan?" Cassy asked, figuring her sister had got stuck with grocery shopping.

"At the market," Emily confirmed. "Now, Jon, there are some bags of ice in the deep freeze in the garage. Chests, beer, wine and soft drinks are stacked against the outer wall. If you'll get all that iced down and onto the back patio, we'll have the drink situation in hand. Cassy, I'm going to let you take over the potato salad, and when you're finished..."

The rest of the afternoon went much the same. The minute any job was completed, Emily had another lined up. Cassy only saw Jon in passing and repeated what she'd told him the night before. "Don't say I didn't warn you." To his credit, he didn't look as if he regretted his decision. Of course, her brothers and sister had yet to make an appearance, and then there was Aunt Effie.

By late afternoon everyone had accomplished the tasks assigned them. The food was ready, picnic tables were set up under the covered patio, a badminton net had been strung between two trees and a croquet court occupied a lighted expanse of grassy lawn between the house and lake.

Shortly after six, guests started arriving. Amidst all the preparations, Cassy and Jon hadn't been able to grab even a few minutes alone. She hoped he wasn't too overwhelmed by the crush of relatives and friends. They were all accustomed to the furor. Jon wasn't.

He'd told her he was an only child and his parents were only children, too. He hadn't grown up surrounded by aunts, uncles and cousins, so he had no concept of how rowdy such a crew could get. She hurried to join him on the patio, determined to stick close by in case she needed to intervene.

Among the first to show up was Alex with their twin great-aunts, Magdalena and Euphemia, in tow. As always, Magda had on a navy serge skirt and white blouse. On her tiny feet were sturdy oxfords with crepe soles. Effie, on the other hand, sported denim and eyelet, complemented by red polka-dot shoes that looked like something from Minnie Mouse's closet.

"Look, Mag," Effie exclaimed as they approached. "Cass has brought a boyfriend. Good-looking, too. Thought she'd end up an old maid like you."

"Hush," Magda scolded in a whisper. "Not every woman is man crazy like you."

"Aunt Magda, Effie, this is Jonathan Manning. He's come with me from Houston."

Magda gave Jon a very proper greeting.

"Well, I should think so," Effie said instead of acknowledging the introductions. "Nasty business, Houston. Can't see why anyone wants to live where the air is thick enough to touch. I was there once, back in the dark ages. Opened the Shamrock Hotel, along with about a thousand others." She cackled and slapped her twin on the arm. "Gave it quite a christening, if memory serves."

"I'm sure you did," Magda said, managing to sound tolerant and disapproving at once. "You've christened a great many things, if memory serves."

Effie ignored her sister's droll comment. "You're a fine, strapping specimen, young man. But your name's too long—"

"Jon," Cassy interrupted, earning a silencing glower from her great-aunt.

"Won't do. Brings back unpleasant memories of my second husband. Or was he the third?" She gave a dismissing wave. "No matter. One wasn't any better than the other." She scrutinized Jon up and down. "Think I'll call you Max."

Cassy let out a little sigh when Jon gave the older woman his most charming smile. "I wish you would, Aunt Effie." He offered her his arm. "May I get you a glass of wine?"

"Sooner have soda pop," she scoffed with a regal toss of her head. "Let's see if we can unearth some bourbon, providing Ed hasn't hid it from me."

Cassy had to laugh at the picture: Effie clinging flirtatiously to Jon's arm; him graciously escorting her into the house.

"Humph," Magda groused. "You better stick to 'im, girl," she advised. "Otherwise Effie's first question will be when he's planning to marry you. After five husbands one would think she'd give up on the institution."

Cassy struck out after the unlikely couple. She didn't doubt Magda's prophecy a bit. To her relief, Kevin and

Meghan had been unaccountably restrained. Even Alex had been reasonably friendly. But Aunt Effie was a wild card.

It turned out she needn't have worried. Effie and Jon had discovered a mutual fondness for the tiny West Indian island of Saba and were trading stories. Since she'd never been there, Cassy's presence was unnecessary.

The rest of the evening continued in that vein. Each time she rushed to rescue him, she found Jon conversing easily on a variety of subjects. No one seemed to find it remarkable that he was with her, nor were there any of the veiled hints about their current—or future—relationship, as she'd expected. He had adapted to the situation like a veteran performer and was accepted with equal ease.

Why had she had misgivings? Cassy asked herself. From the beginning she'd felt that she and Jon were destined to be together. Fitting in with her family and friends was an extension of that. It was natural that they be here, sharing the closeness.

With Jon at her side, Cassy relaxed during the bountiful meal. Her mother always supplied twice as much food as the guest list demanded, then everyone else brought more.

Long-established tradition ended the feast with two birthday cakes, each with the appropriate number of candles. Cassy looked into Jon's eyes, made a wish and, with an impressive huff, blew out every one on her cake.

He smiled, and she took it as an omen.

At dusk the lights were turned on and the more active gravitated toward the games. Cassy and Jon ended up on the croquet court with a group of her cousins who were particularly competitive. Through the first set of wickets, etiquette was observed. After that it was gloves off. On the back side, Cassy had a clear shot at either the wicket or Jon's ball. She chose the latter. With a vengeance, she sent it flying out of position.

"Mercenary little witch," he muttered in an undertone as he stalked toward his ball. "You're gonna pay for that."

The glint in his eyes and the familiar way his mouth opened when he focused on hers left no doubt that his retribution would come later. In private. Cassy welcomed it, but she was having such a glorious time she wanted to keep the mock feud going. Her lips formed an astonished O. "I had no idea you'd be such a poor sport."

"'Poor sport,' my butt. You weren't trying for the wicket. You aimed straight for my ball. Why?"

She smiled ingenuously. "Maybe I wanted to get a rise out of you."

Cassy loved his devilish laugh. "Count on it, honey."

Long after midnight, under a blanket on the deck of the sailboat, Jon exacted his revenge. "If this is punishment," Cassy breathed, soaring to the outer limits of pleasure, "I'm going to be naughty every chance I get. And hope I have to pay like this."

The rest of the weekend passed much too quickly. Still, she was happy because it had gone so well. Jon and her father had talked fishing; with Meghan he had discussed business. And once or twice she'd caught her mother beaming at them.

WHEN THEY GOT BACK TO HOUSTON, less than a week remained before Cassy departed for Honduras. Now that leaving was imminent, the enthusiasm she had felt since her project's inception returned full force. Jon had often diverted her temporarily. There had even been a few occasions when she'd wished she didn't have to go at all.

But this was Cassy's dream. She believed in it. At times she'd wanted it so badly she had been driven to forget everything else in her life. And within days she would be there to see the first concrete steps taken to make her dream a reality.

She didn't expect Jon to share all her ideals. It was imperative that he understand them, though. He vowed that he did. He still didn't want her to go. No argument, regardless of how valid or sound it was, could convince Jon that Cassy would come back to him unharmed and unchanged.

Every night she'd tried to console him. But with each passing day he became more agitated. Finally, their last night together arrived, and she almost dreaded it. Something told her Jon would pull out all the stops. He had nothing to lose. Though Cassy knew she wouldn't, couldn't, relent, the rift was making her miserable.

All the arrangements had been made, and she'd said goodbye to all her friends, telling them not to call or come by for any reason that night. She planned to cook dinner at home and spend a quiet evening with Jon. For her, tomorrow would begin at dawn and not end until many hours and miles later.

Nervousness coiled her insides when she went to answer the knock at her door. She knew it was Jon. But for some reason he'd chosen not to use the key she had given him. That simple omission unnerved her further. They hadn't been truly relaxed since returning

The Reluctant Bachelor

from Minnesota. The distance between them was widening. One look told her that tonight he was more remote than ever.

"Come in," she said, standing aside. "You look tired. Hard day?"

"Aren't they all?" He walked past her, then started, as if he'd done something wrong. Turning, he bent slightly and kissed her, but it wasn't well aimed, and it was done almost by rote.

In the living room he roamed restlessly, like an animal unable to find the right place to settle. "I thought about bringing wine. But I figured you wouldn't want to drink before a long trip like that. I could have gotten flowers, but you'd just have to throw them out." He lifted his shoulders in apology. "I couldn't think of anything you need."

"Your being here is enough. That's all I need."

"I wish that were true."

"It *is* true, Jon. I wish I could make you believe it." Dismayed, she watched him trudge over to the plumeria, one of its tiny yellow blossoms dwarfed when he cupped it in his big hand.

"I think I had some kind of mistaken idea that a stupid gift would charm you. Make me seem—" he looked at her and gave another helpless shrug "—romantic, I guess."

"The gift was not stupid," she asserted vehemently. "It was charming and thoughtful and romantic." She went over to him then and shook his arm. "I'd love you without gifts. But that doesn't mean I'm not happy to get them. I'm flattered that you were thinking about me at all."

"Lately, you're all I do think about." He wrapped her in his arms and held her so tightly against him she could feel the steady meter of his heartbeat.

Being this close to Jon usually brought joy and a thrilling sense of rightness. Tonight she could feel despair weighing heavily on both of them. If she wasn't careful, the whole tone of the evening could turn maudlin, and that wouldn't do either of them any good. Cassy pulled away and led him into the kitchen.

"Hope you're hungry. I've made some of your favorites." Because she liked doing it, she had fixed quite a few meals for Jon and found him remarkably unpicky. Discovering that she was a good cook had seemed to surprise and please him. But not as much as learning that she liked meat loaf and mashed potatoes. He'd jokingly confessed to thinking rich folks ate caviar and lobster three times a day. Personally, she couldn't stand caviar, and though lobster was delicious, it gave her hives.

He dished up the fettuccine with smoked salmon while she finished the Caesar salad and removed whole-wheat rolls from the oven.

"You're the only person I know who bakes," he said, sniffing the rolls. "How come?"

"How come you don't know anyone else who bakes?"

"No, why do you bother?" Together they carried the food into the dining room. "Is it worth all the time it takes?"

"You bet. One of my grandmothers was a terrific cook. And since I've always been a pig, I hung around her kitchen a lot. I guess some of it rubbed off."

But Cassy's appetite deserted her, and Jon's wasn't much better. They both rearranged more food than they ate. She didn't even offer the fresh raspberries. After the requisite amount of time, they left the dishes on the table and went back to the living room. As he had on more than one occasion, Jon chose a chair instead of the sofa.

She went to the stereo, set the volume low and pushed in a Beethoven cassette, thinking some ponderous Wagner would probably better reflect the mood. "Would you like an after-dinner drink? Some coffee or tea?"

"No. Well, maybe I could use a brandy," he said, surging to his feet. "I'll get it." He took an inordinate amount of time locating the decanter and glass, as if anything were preferable to sitting down face-to-face.

Cassy decided to confront him head-on. "Remember that first time? At the lodge?"

His eyes blazed, and she knew it was unnecessary to elaborate about which time. "As if I could ever forget."

"I feel a little bit like that now. Knowing what I want, but nervous at the prospect of getting it."

Jon curved his palms around the glass and stared into it. "Cassy, I'm not so sure it's a good idea to bring up sex. Not at this point. There are other things that need to be discussed."

"'Sex'!" she shouted, frustrated because she knew what he was going to bring up and that there would be no solution. "Pardon me while I get my terms straight. Here I've been thinking that what we shared was making love. Now you say it was sex. Well, I guess men always have a different, less idealized view of... coupling." She emphasized the last word, making it sound as sordid as possible.

"Stop it! Stop goading me!" His brandy sloshed close to the snifter's rim. "You know I didn't mean that."

Cassy sank back against the cushions, depleted by her outburst. "Unfortunately, Jonathan, I *don't* know what you mean. I don't know how you feel. And I don't know what you want."

With extreme care Jon set down his glass without ever having taken a drink. For weeks he'd relied on a series of sound reasons to keep her from going to Honduras. Logic and facts hadn't deterred her. Hunched forward, elbows resting on his knees, gaze locked on hers, he played the only card he had. "For starters, I want you to not get on that plane tomorrow."

She looked as if he had struck her, and Jon felt a corresponding pain. He hated doing this, but he was desperate. He would try any means available to keep her from leaving him. She shook her head, unable to speak.

"I'm asking you not to go to Honduras, Cassy," he repeated, this time the request more imperative.

A flush of indignation spread across her cheekbones. "What gives you the right? I've never demanded anything of you, never even asked for much. Whatever you gave, it was because you wanted to. Do you think you're in the position to expect me to give up a dream?"

"No, I honestly don't. I have no rights."

"Yet you're asking me not to go when you know I have to. You say you understand my dedication to seeing this through, say you understand why I can't turn my back on something I've invested everything in. Then you turn around and expect the impossible."

"If I were operating on intellect alone, I'd agree with you. But my feelings, my emotions are involved here, and I've discovered them to be quite irrational."

"What are they telling you?"

"They are screaming to hold on to you, to keep you from leaving me. That if I don't, this is goodbye."

"Jon, I wish I could fathom why you're so troubled over my being gone for a few weeks. I have to believe that we're dealing with something more basic than time spent apart. But I can't fight what I don't understand."

"To put it simply, I'm afraid I haven't given you enough to come back to." How many times had he damned his inability to say three simple words and prove to Cassy how much she meant to him? Now he feared he'd waited too long.

"But I love you. Nothing you have or haven't done will keep me from getting back to you as fast as possible. Can't you see that?"

"Irrational emotions, remember? I'm eaten up with them. Like those rights we were talking about. Those I haven't earned. I want them anyway. What would give me those rights, Cassy?" he taunted. "My saying I love you? Would that keep you from going?"

"Now you're goading me," she snapped.

"No, I'm not," he said quietly, earnestly. "I'm telling you I love you. Cassy, I love you."

Cassy's hand flew to her throat, where she felt her heart tapping out a message of thanksgiving. "Oh, Jonathan, you'll never know how much I've wanted to hear that." This should have been the shining golden moment of her life. But like gold tainted by impurities, it was less than perfect. The circumstances made her question the timing of Jon's declaration of love. She knew he wasn't the type to frivolously toss out such statements. But his desperation had been steadily increasing. To what extremes might a desperate man go? "Are you sure you mean it?"

"There have been so many times I wanted to say it. You must have sensed that. But the words always stuck in my throat. I kept telling myself that when it was right, they'd come out easily. And they did. I've never said it before, never felt this way about any woman." He came to her, touching her cheek with the back of his fingers. "Yes, honey, I'm sure."

Cassy looked into his eyes with a silent appeal. *Then please don't use it as a weapon against me. Don't issue an ultimatum. Don't make me choose between Honduras and your love.*

He looked away, saying nothing. Cassy released a sigh that was almost painful. At least he hadn't forced her to make an unthinkable choice. But they were both in a no-win situation. From the way Jon's shoulders slumped, it was obvious that he knew it, too. Still, she wanted to leave him with something, show him that she was willing to compromise in deference to his feelings.

"I've been thinking," she began, drawing his gaze back to her. "After about two weeks, I can probably get away, at least for a while, and come back to Houston."

Cassy hadn't expected him to dance with glee, but her concession didn't seem to encourage him at all. "That would be good. If you can manage it." He didn't sound as if he believed she'd really come back, or that it would make any difference if she did.

After so many futile attempts, she saw that there was simply no way to convince him with words. The proof would have to come with her return. "I love you," she whispered. "And we'll be together in two weeks. What do you want from me now?"

His head tipped back slightly, lids narrowed so she couldn't quite read the message in his eyes. "I want you to make love to me, Cassy."

His request aroused her primitive, womanly instincts and filled her with daring. "Shall I carry you off to bed . . . or take you—"

"Here . . ."

She slowly removed his suit coat and flung it aside. Her hands skipped over the tautening muscles of his shoulders, back, arms. A heavy groan came from deep in his chest. The sound inflamed her like the most potent aphrodisiac. She made a fist around his tie and pulled his mouth down to within a breath of touching hers as she undid the knot.

The length of silk landed atop his jacket with a soft plop. Then the buttons of his shirt fell victim to her nimble fingers. Cassy rubbed her cheek over the silky hair that covered his chest and inhaled deeply. "You smell . . . not quite civilized. No cologne. Like a man." Her tongue swirled around one of his nipples in a pagan rhythm of seduction.

"Ah, Cassy. I'm—You'd better stop."

"No," she murmured, peeling the shirt from him, "not yet." She eased him down on the couch and removed his shoes. She'd barely begun to make love to him, and already Jon was boldly, excitingly aroused. So was she. Cassy gloried in her femininity, certain only she could spark this immediate, insistent need in her man.

She stood before him and began unfastening her clothes. It didn't occur to her to attempt a slow strip-tease—they were both beyond subtlety. But through sensually lowered lashes, she saw that with every button she freed, the tension in Jon heightened. His bare chest rose and fell rapidly.

After skimming off her skirt and blouse, she took a step toward him, clad only in silk and lace. Cassy knelt at Jon's feet. But she didn't feel subservient. She felt powerful. She reached to unclasp his belt and pants. Even before she touched the zipper, Cassy felt how hard he was, how full. But tugging off his remaining clothing and seeing it confirmed made her breathless. "Oh, Jon, you're so—"

"Come here, Cassy. . . ." He removed her teddy and bikini and pulled her onto his lap facing him. Nude in the lamplight, astride him, Cassy felt very wild, very wanton. She slid her tongue into his mouth, and he moaned at the evocative possession before matching the rhythm of her quick, hard thrusts.

Both his hands moved to her breasts, covering them completely. Hot sensations coursed through her, so sharp that she had to drag her lips from his in order to breathe. She looked down, hypnotized by the contrast of his large, dark hands moving on her fairer skin. Watching the gentle squeezing motions was intensely stimulating, and Cassy felt her nipples bead against his palms.

She wanted his mouth there, but instead he found the valley between her breasts and sucked lightly. When her nipples were tight and aching, and she couldn't bear the deprivation any longer, she guided his mouth to where she needed it. But the delicate finesse of his tongue only fanned the flames in both of them.

Jon's hands outlined the shape of her waist and hips before his thumbs came to rest along the crease where legs and body joined. Fingers flexing on her outer thighs, he established a cadence that reverberated through Cassy like shock waves. She stiffened and cried out when his thumbs inched together to merge at the most sensitive spot on her body.

"Jon-a-than."

"The way you say that drives me wild."

He stroked through her flowing heat, and Cassy gasped. She moved to ease the tormenting pressure he was building, but there was no escape from the magic of his thumbs.

"Come closer, honey. Closer. I want you now. We're both so ready." His hands cradled her bottom. "That's it. Lift." Her hand reached down to shape, then guide him as he eased inside her. "Ah, Cassy. Perfect. Now take what you want."

He had commanded her to love him; now she could set the tempo and govern his movements. But he'd driven her to a fever pitch, and dominance no longer mattered. They were too caught up in the tightly escalating spiral of passion. Jon's lack of control pushed her past the boundaries of restraint until the need for satisfaction consumed her.

Unable to deny herself any longer, she wanted him to come with her. "Jon, I can't wait."

Jon's hips pumped wildly, and her body rocked from the force of his release. She let go and rode the pulsing current of vibrations until she found her own. Cassy wasn't sure if the scream was real or inside her head. Or if it mattered.

"I love you," he said, his hand on her heart as it began to slow its frantic beating.

Her hand rested on his heart. "And I love you."

They had that to bind them, and a hurtful conflict to separate them. Lovemaking had not changed that. Neither had expected that it would.

"Cassy, I don't want to hide how I feel any longer. I'm disappointed that love's not enough to keep you with me. Frustrated that I can't bend you to my will. Angry because I can't force you to stay. I know you're experiencing the same feelings." His forehead bumped against hers. "It was probably a mistake to make love with so much unresolved. Unfair to both of us."

Cassy clamped her eyes shut tightly. "Jonathan, in love, all's fair."

"No, if that were the case, we wouldn't be facing this problem."

He gently lifted her from him and reached for his slacks. Feeling bereft and chilled, Cassy gathered her clothes and went to the bedroom for a robe. When she came back, he was dressed and finishing the brandy.

He looked at her for a long time before asking softly, "Nothing I say will make a difference, will it? You're going."

"Yes."

"Then I've got to get out of here. I can't stay."

She followed him to the door. "Why, Jon?"

"Right now I'm feeling desperate enough that I'd do anything—*anything*—to keep you here. And, afterward, I think we'd both be sorry."

12

JON STARED MOROSELY at the tray he'd filled in the cafeteria line. He stopped here often on his way from work because the food was good and tasted like home cooking. Cassy had fixed him meals like this, and eaten with her in her cozy, cluttered apartment, the food had tasted better than any gourmet fare.

Cassy was gone. Had been for five days. The longest five days of Jon's life. He'd gone to the office early and stayed late in an attempt to pretend he wasn't desolate without her. But he was. Of course, he'd admitted that he would miss her. He just hadn't counted on being unable to function without her.

Jon automatically lifted his fork at intervals, determined to eat every bite. Accomplishing that ordinary task would be the first thing he'd successfully completed all week. But he couldn't escape from his thoughts. In the beginning he'd told himself that by getting on the plane, Cassy had made her choice. And that in the crunch, her choice hadn't been him. After spending a wretched first night without her, he knew it wasn't so simple. She had repeatedly and steadfastly claimed that Jon was the most important thing in her life. Still, her love for him didn't preclude other duties and responsibilities. Cassy was being sensible and realistic. For the first time in his life, Jon was the one behaving illogically. He recognized the problem, just didn't know how to solve it.

He tried to visualize Cassy in Honduras, working alongside the volunteers, watching her dream put into operation. When he'd told her he understood her need to see it through, it was true. But his own need for her was so great that he couldn't think of anything or anyone that took precedence over Cassy. She had become his whole world. What did a man do when he reached that state?

His father's favorite saying fit the current situation to a T: fish or cut bait. He was compelled to make the decision soon.

Jon had just congratulated himself on the small victory over his entrée and vegetables and was about to attack a fruit salad when a family sitting down at a nearby table caught his attention. He could see the man's face clearly and didn't recognize him. The woman's back was to him, but something seemed familiar about her. Between them a toddler sat in a high chair, diving immediately into a dish of red Jell-O cubes. Jon put down his fork and continued to study them, unaccountably spellbound by the tableau.

When the mother rose to retie the little girl's bib, Jon pushed his dishes aside and planted his elbows on the table. No wonder she'd looked familiar. It was Julie, a woman he'd been involved with a few years back. Now she was married, had a daughter and, as evidenced by her profile, was expecting another baby soon. He stared unashamedly, drawn in by how easily the couple talked with each other, stopping often to smile at their child's antics. Witnessing their closeness, their obvious happiness triggered an unfamiliar sensation he couldn't quite define. Not jealousy, certainly, for he and Julie had made a mutual decision to part and had done it as friends. He wished her only the best.

So why did seeing her happy make *him* feel empty and deprived? He continued to watch the other table while he analyzed the strangely emotional reaction for cause. Finally it hit him. He was projecting himself into a similar scene featuring Cassy. If he couldn't give her what she needed and had to let her go, someone else could take his place. Marry her. Give her children. The thought of Cassy finding that fulfillment with another man ate at his insides like acid.

Jon had had several long-lasting relationships with women that he'd found satisfying and worthwhile. He'd liked them, respected them, told himself he could learn to love them. But the relationships had all ended because the women eventually wanted more. A proposal. And while he understood that, he'd never been able to offer what they wanted. It was as if some integral ingredient were missing, rendering him unable to commit himself permanently to one person.

Then he'd met Cassy.

After knowing her for a few weeks, he had taken the plunge and confessed his love. A major step for him, to be sure, but not enough for the long haul. He wanted to give Cassy everything she deserved, and in Jon's mind that included marriage to go with the love. To accept that as the next logical step would require probing deeply into old wounds, wounds he'd believed had healed so long ago that not even the trace of a scar remained. He saw now that for more than twenty years they hadn't been forgotten, just skillfully concealed. A core of residual bitterness remained, and he'd allowed that to deprive him of what most men took for granted.

Was he going to sentence himself to a lifetime of watching other men build a future with their wives and families? Or was he going to do something concrete to secure his own? Jon got up from the table, forgetting the vow to finish his food. He was going home to do some heavy soul-searching. Not to his condo, which seemed lonely and empty, but to Cassy's apartment, where, surrounded by reminders of her, he could set a new course for his life. And when she returned to him as she'd promised, he intended to greet her with good news.

He was unlocking his car when he heard someone call his name. Mother Divine. No, in her beige linen suit and knotted hair, this was Helen, the insurance tycoon. He returned her wave and walked over several rows to join her. Odd how he didn't find her at all disconcerting after being around her a few times. In that cantina he'd almost panicked when she had read his palm. Now he wasn't so sure that her prediction hadn't been right on the mark. How quickly his life had changed since knowing Cassy.

"Eating alone?" Helen's brows arched inquiringly. "Counting the days, perhaps?"

"Yes to both. Too bad you didn't get here sooner. You could have spared me another solitary meal."

"And possibly have reassured you that Charlotte will rush back to your welcoming arms." She echoed his faint smile. "She will, you know. She's quite taken with you."

The Reluctant Bachelor

Jon's smile broadened when he recalled Cassy's frequent declarations of love. "So she says. I think you might have suspected something like that would happen the first time you saw us together."

"I picked up several vibrations that night. Two of them came across very strongly. The first was your reluctance to accept the budding attraction you felt for Charlotte. It would have been obvious even to someone whose powers of perception are far weaker than mine."

Jon couldn't dispute that. He'd fought it early and for as long as he could, but in the end it hadn't mattered. "And the second?"

"Why, that there was nothing either of you could do to stop it, of course. It was predestined." Helen looked down at her watch. "I've got to run," she said, heading toward the cafeteria. "I don't want to keep my dinner date waiting."

Jon chuckled and wished her well, then walked to his car.

As he drove away, he felt more positive than he had in days. Hearing Helen confirm Cassy's devotion to him revived his battered spirits. That gnawing fear that she wouldn't come back was dissipating. In nine days it would be gone. In the meantime, Jon was going to spend those days planning one hell of a reunion.

But eight days later his reunion plans were in shambles, and he was in even worse shape. Early that morning a wire from Cassy had been delivered to his office. The message said only, "I love you. Unable to return as planned. Stand by."

In those initial minutes after reading it, Jon had reacted like a wild man. Every dreadful consequence he'd imagined before she left—plus a few even more horrible ones—ricocheted inside his head. When he at last got himself calmed down enough to reread the wire, he decided to rule out the more gruesome possibilities. Cassy had not been kidnapped or murdered. Had something like that happened, she couldn't have sent a telegram. Nor was this the equivalent of a Dear John letter. He knew she would never do that to him.

He was left to mull over the more plausible reasons for her staying in Honduras. She could be ill. The wire had said "unable," but she probably hadn't meant it literally. That left the simplest, most logical of all conclusions. Something to do with the project required her attention. Jon decided to operate on that premise, since he couldn't bear to contemplate any of the other explanations. She might not even be delayed that long. She'd said to "stand by." That must mean she planned to contact him soon. That made perfect sense, he told himself.

But he couldn't wait.

Jon had the airline on the phone within seconds. There was one flight a day, departing in about two hours. Luckily he kept an overnight bag and a few extra clothes at the office. His passport was in the safe, and he could get cash at the bank in the lobby downstairs. Once at the airport, he could pick up the required tourist card. Just under four hours after takeoff, he would be in Tegucigalpa. How he'd go about locating Cassy once he got there wasn't firm in his mind yet. But he would find her. He had to.

More than twenty-four hours later, Jon was still reciting the same mantra. It had taken hours before he'd finally run Alex to ground, hastily explained his mission and was rewarded with the handshake that had been withheld when they found him in Cassy's bedroom. Jon gritted his teeth through too many delays, but at last they piled into a dilapidated Jeep and took off for the interior highlands, where the volunteers had set up a command post of sorts. Alex had readily agreed to help him track down Cassy, and after being together constantly since then, each had reformed his opinion of the other. Cassy, however, had stayed a step ahead of them.

Alex ground the gears, a chronic habit, and they careened around a corner into a small mountain settlement. Squawking chickens scattered in all directions; feathers flew. Women and children scurried out of small thatched-roof adobe huts. And there stood Cassy, wielding a syringe that was big enough to baste a turkey and vaccinating a mean-looking cow. The scene was so ludicrous, his relief so great, that Jon burst out laughing.

Cassy looked up, so stunned to see Jonathan with Alex that at first she wrote it off as an hallucination. She had missed him so much, wanted to see him so badly that her starving imagination must have conjured him up. But she didn't think hallucinations laughed or called her name... or gathered her up in hard embraces. This one felt like, smelled like, tasted like..."Jon?"

He kissed her then, with all the passionate fire any woman could want from her man. Cassy sensed a small audience gathering in a circle around them. This was an especially remote settlement, not even large enough to be classed as a village. Jon and Alex's arrival along with Cassy's presence was more activity than the residents had seen in years, and they were curious. She smiled at them, conveying that there was nothing to be concerned about.

"What on earth are you doing here, Jonathan?"

His arm was around her, as if he planned to hang on to her for a long time. "I came to be with you until you're ready to go home." At her astonished look, he added, "I couldn't last another day without seeing you. I have something to say—to ask, really—that can't wait."

"What is it?" A ribbon of excitement unfurled in her stomach.

"Uh, I hadn't figured on asking in front of an audience. I guess it can wait a little longer, although I'm not sure I can." He gestured toward Alex, who was circulating among the populace, notebook in hand. "In the meantime, do you think your brother will notice if I drag you into the forest and make love to you for three or four days nonstop?"

"Three or four days might be iffy. But I'll bet we can get by with an hour or two later this evening. Will you settle for that?"

"Honey, the way I'm aching, I'd settle for a quickie behind the nearest pine tree."

Cassy laughed. "So impatient."

"Damn right!"

"This doesn't sound like the old Jonathan, the one who wanted to take everything slow."

"That guy is gone. Done in by a fast little number with a braid and a sassy—"

"Mouth?" she asked, cutting him off.

"Yeah, mouth." He kissed her again. "Guess I'll have to be content with that for a while, huh?"

Cassy could almost feel Jonathan's eagerness erupting from him. It was contagious. But it was crucial not to offend the people she'd come to help, so she introduced Jon, explaining that he was her *amigo* from America. What a tame description for all he was to her. Still, she couldn't flaunt him as her *amante*. Lover. If the choice was hers, she'd be calling him *marido*—husband.

He stayed close by, observing while she finished inoculating the small herd, asking questions. When the task was completed, the villagers insisted on sharing their evening meal. Refusing would have been unthinkable, so the sun was setting by the time Jon and Cassy were able to excuse themselves and start back to the larger town where Cassy's group was headquartered.

Alex gunned his battered Jeep after saying he'd look for them when he saw them. His sly look at Cassy said, "I know something you don't." And his attitude toward Jon had definitely improved.

Cassy and Jon took her Jeep, and they bounced along the narrow, rutted road for about five miles before she stopped and switched off the ignition. She angled herself to face him, one hand still draped over the steering wheel. "You've been driving me up the wall since that announcement you made earlier. Now I'm the one who can't wait."

He looked at the decrepit vehicle, then gazed up at the soaring conifers all around them. "This is one fantasy that I'd never have come up with on my own." He grinned wryly and lifted her hand. "I guess it's appropriate, in a perverted sort of way. I haven't done anything by the rule book since meeting you."

She dampened her lips and said boldly, "There are times when other forces take over. Rules don't apply when two people fall in love."

"So I've learned." Jon fidgeted, eagerness and reluctance etched eloquently on his face.

Cassy threaded their fingers together and smiled her encouragement. "Whatever you have to tell or ask me can't be all that intimidating. It's just me."

"That's why it's so important to do this right. Because it is you. Nothing else has ever mattered so much." His fingers tightened, and she felt them shaking.

"Charlotte Cassidy Laurens, will you marry me?"

Cassy's eyes closed for a few seconds to absorb the moment's perfection. His words meant everything to her because of what he'd overcome in order to say them. "Jonathan, I love you. And I'd love to marry you. But are you—" Relief and love and certainty were mirrored in his eyes, halting her question. "Of course you're sure," she breathed. "You'd never ask if you weren't."

"I was so scared I wondered if I'd be able to speak at all." He yanked out a handkerchief and mopped his face. "Luckily, you accepted the first time. I don't think I'd survive doing this again." He chuckled, and suddenly his nervousness fled. "I had the reunion all planned. It was going to be so romantic you'd be swept off your feet. Instead, here I am dirty and sweaty, proposing in a Jeep." His palm framed her cheek. "But when your telegram came, I got so shook up I forgot everything except getting here as fast as possible."

"You're about the last person I expected to see when I heard the Jeep pull up." She laid her hand over his, reveling in the gentle touch almost as much as his words. "Oh, Jon. I'm so glad you're here. I've missed you." Her teeth sank into her lower lip when she remembered their agonized parting. "I was so afraid that after I left, you'd decide I wasn't worth the trouble." His look of utter disgust silenced that argument.

"Let's get out of this bucket. I want to kiss you, and I can't do it with that damned gearshift between us."

Simultaneously they opened their doors, got out and came together behind the Jeep. He had been right. Two weeks was too long to go without the feel of his strong, vital body pressed to hers, without the sweet warmth of his taste filling her mouth. From the beginning, the lightest brush of Jon's lips had drawn her into a shimmering snare of passion. With his promise for the future echoing inside her head, the lure was more powerful than ever. His kisses inspired an ache to yield, a need to give. Her mouth opened beneath his, tongues touched and mated in a frenzy of unleashed desire that went on and on. Only when they were both breathless could they bear to break the bond.

"That helped a lot." In the fading twilight Jon smiled down at her, lids narrowed with sexy intent. "But not enough to hold me until we get home."

Cassy looked up at him through half-closed lashes. "We're going to have to get extremely creative. I have a tent to myself, but it's really small and..."

"I know. So close to the other tents that you can hear a whisper. God, Cassy, I can't love you without talking, without moaning. And you make the most incredible sounds when you—"

"If you don't stop talking like that, you're going to be hearing those sounds before you expect it." She shuddered against him. "There's a blanket in the back of the Jeep. Feel brave enough to bed down on the forest floor?"

He was already digging in the back. "I don't know about brave. Those damn fleas at the health center nearly ate me alive last night. But I'm hot enough to risk even that."

The conifers grew so close together that it was hard to find enough space to spread the blanket. Desire provided such a potent motivator that they knelt immediately, facing each other.

"Cassy, I'd like to be a gentleman, a polished lover who'd take his time and be gentle." His hands were already caressing her breasts. "But there's no way I'm going to bring that off this time."

She covered his face with damp, feverish kisses. "That's not what I need. I want you too much."

Their clothing was tossed aside in haste, and they joined in a burst of longing that flared brightly. Jon was inside her, Cassy was around him, and their mutual hunger was quickly assuaged. Within minutes they were wrapped together, oblivious to the setting, lazing in the aftermath of shared pleasure.

"That was a spectacular reunion," Cassy said, idly massaging his back. "But I have to admit I'm curious about your sudden change of heart. Happy, but curious."

The play of his lips over her shoulders was more affectionate than sensual. "Would you believe it took place after seeing an old flame?"

Cassy pretended a pout that was lost in the near darkness. "I'm not sure I want to hear this."

"I only saw her from a distance, and she was with her husband and little girl. They looked very contented, very glad to be together. Then the next day I ran into Christie, Pat's wife. We talked about being able to have a successful marriage even though one of the partners has to be gone a lot. She told me something that really hit home. She said in the final analysis, you love someone and you take what you get. Forget all the reasons why it won't work, because none of them matter."

Her hand stopped its lazy caressing. "And those two events were enough to convince you that you want to get married?"

"No, enough to convince me to evaluate why I've been so set against it for all these years." One hand came up to frame her neck; his thumb tipped up her chin. "I love you, Cassy."

"You say it so easily now." And the words were more precious to her with every repetition.

"Suddenly, it seems like the most natural thing in the world. I can't imagine not saying it."

Cassy adjusted herself to see him better. His face was dusky with the approaching night, but the conviction there was easy to read. "What made it so difficult before?"

"An old story." He glanced away as if summoning his nerve, then looked back at her. "You probably wondered why I acted like such an ass over your money."

"It did seem excessive."

"All my life I've avoided wealthy women. My mother was rich."

"Was?"

"I don't know her at all. Wouldn't recognize the woman if she walked up to me this minute. She left when I was six, and I have almost no memory of her. I did grow up with one overriding impression. She didn't want her husband. She didn't want her son. And her wealthy family was only too willing to pay for the privilege of getting rid of us."

Cassy gasped, enraged by the unforgivable cruelty. She felt him stiffen, but he didn't withdraw. "I don't have to know this now, if you'd rather not talk about it." She crossed her fingers that he wouldn't accept the offer.

"No, I want to tell you and then put it in the past.... My father remarried when I was twelve. My stepmother was a school counselor, and she got me to talk about my feelings toward my mother. I thought I'd come to terms with them, but there were obviously some things left unresolved. What I didn't realize was that I unconsciously let something that happened when I was six filter over into all my relationships with women. Until you, I needed to maintain a certain distance and control over my emotions. I guess I equated love with rejection, so I didn't risk it. Sounds pretty convoluted now, even dumb. I know one thing for sure. All that's behind me, and where I am now feels great."

Cassy felt positively lighthearted for the first time in days. She shared her elation with a hug. "Where you are *is* great. You're right where you belong. I think I'll keep you here for a long, long time."

He dropped a small peck on her nose. "Know what I think? I think I'd like to make love with my future wife so I can show her how much that means to me."

"I always knew you were a clever man, Jonathan."

"THERE'S A CERTAIN JUSTICE here," Jon said later that night after they'd bid everyone good-night and stuffed themselves into Cassy's tiny tent. "I've just got myself engaged to a woman with millions, and we're sleeping in a one-man tent."

"One-person," Cassy corrected, glowing because he could now joke about her money. "Look at it this way. It will be a fantastic story to tell our grandchildren." She held her breath, waiting.

He laughed. "Mother Divine said three children. She didn't take it any further than that."

There was no way a mortal woman could be any happier than she was at this moment. "Guess we'll just have to leave it up to the younger generation to figure that one out." Luckily the mountain night was cool enough that they could snuggle tightly together, the way she wanted to sleep every night from now on. And she would be able to. Gabe had called her at dawn the day she left Houston with the news she'd been waiting to hear. Being able to tell Jon that her traveling would be drastically reduced was icing on the cake now that he'd decided he could accept it without being threatened. "Jonathan, you've given me everything I want. As much as I can, I'll try to do the same for you."

"I know you'll need to come back here often in the future, Cassy. But I'm giving you notice right now. You're not coming unless I can come with you." Her fingers tightened on his waist. "Hell, I can learn to vaccinate a cow as well as the next guy. Chickens, too, if necessary."

"Do you realize what you're saying?"

"Of course, I do. I'm not sure how I was fortunate enough to find you, but I'll do anything to keep you. I'm not about to question my good luck."

Cassy smiled against his lips. Let him think it was luck. She believed in luck, too, although more often than not you had to make your own. But Cassy knew they'd had a little extra help.

Fate had given her Jonathan, and she planned to treasure the gift for the rest of their lives.

EDITOR'S CHOICE

TIFFANY WHITE

OPEN INVITATION

A deliciously scented pink envelope... a few naughty suggestions... and a man left aching for the woman behind the words.

Tiffany White redefines the art of seduction, proving that a woman's imagination... and a man's interpretation... are their most sensuous assets.

Harlequin Temptation and Tiffany White are offering you an Open Invitation to eroticism. It's yours in November.

HARLEQUIN
Temptation

You'll flip... your pages won't!
Read paperbacks *hands-free* with

Book Mate • I

The perfect "mate" for all your romance paperbacks

Traveling • Vacationing • At Work • In Bed • Studying • Cooking • Eating

Perfect size for all standard paperbacks, this wonderful invention makes reading a pure pleasure! Ingenious design holds paperback books OPEN and FLAT so even wind can't ruffle pages — leaves your hands free to do other things. Reinforced, wipe-clean vinyl-covered holder flexes to let you turn pages without undoing the strap... supports paperbacks so well, they have the strength of hardcovers!

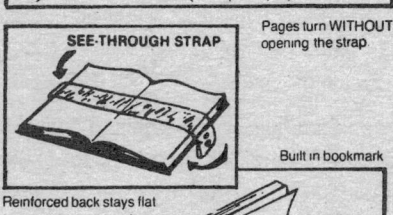

Pages turn WITHOUT opening the strap

SEE-THROUGH STRAP

Reinforced back stays flat

Built in bookmark

BOOK MARK

BACK COVER HOLDING STRIP

10 x 7¼ opened
Snaps closed for easy carrying, too

Available now. Send your name, address, and zip code, along with a check or money order for just $5.95 + .75¢ for postage & handling (for a total of $6.70) payable to Reader Service to:

Reader Service
Bookmate Offer
901 Fuhrmann Blvd.
P.O. Box 1396
Buffalo, N.Y. 14269-1396

Offer not available in Canada
*New York and Iowa residents add appropriate sales tax.

BM-G

COMING IN OCTOBER

Janet DAILEY

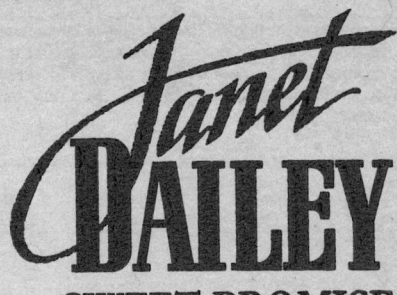

SWEET PROMISE

Erica made two serious mistakes in Mexico. One was taking Rafael de la Torres for a gigolo, the other was assuming that the scandal of marrying him would get her father's attention. Her father wasn't interested, and Erica ran home to Texas the next day, keeping her marriage a secret. She knew she'd have to find Rafael someday to get a divorce, but she didn't expect to run into him at a party—and she was amazed to discover that her "gigolo" was the head of a powerful family, and deeply in love with her....

Watch for this bestselling Janet Dailey favorite, coming in October from Harlequin.

JAN-PROM-1

Indulge a Little, Give a Lot

To receive your free gift send us the required number of proofs-of-purchase from any specially marked "Indulge A Little" Harlequin or Silhouette book with the Offer Certificate properly completed, plus a cheque or money order (do not send cash) to cover postage and handling payable to Harlequin/Silhouette "Indulge A Little, Give A Lot" Offer. We will send you the specified gift.

Mail-in-Offer

OFFER CERTIFICATE

Item:	A. Collector's Doll	B. Soaps in a Basket	C. Potpourri Sachet	D. Scented Hangers
# of Proofs-of-Purchase	18	12	6	4
Postage & Handling	$3.25	$2.75	$2.25	$2.00
Check One				

Name _____
Address _____ Apt. # _____
City _____ State _____ Zip _____

Indulge A LITTLE GIVE A LOT

ONE PROOF OF PURCHASE

To collect your free gift by mail you must include the necessary number of proofs-of-purchase plus postage and handling with offer certificate.

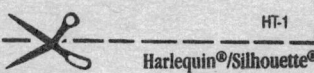

HT-1

Harlequin®/Silhouette®

Mail this certificate, designated number of proofs-of-purchase and check or money order for postage and handling to:

**INDULGE A LITTLE
P.O. Box 9055 Buffalo, N.Y. 14269-9055**

NOTE THIS IMPORTANT OFFER'S TERMS

Offer available in the United States and Canada.

Requests must be postmarked by February 28, 1990. Only proofs-of-purchase from specially marked "Indulge A Little" Harlequin or Silhouette books will be accepted. This certificate must accompany your request and may not be reproduced in any manner. Offer void where prohibited, taxed or restricted by law. LIMIT ONE GIFT PER NAME, FAMILY, GROUP, ORGANIZATION OR ADDRESS. Please allow up to 8 weeks after receipt of order for shipment. Offer good while quantities last. Collector's dolls will be mailed to first 15,000 qualifying submitters. All other submitters will receive 18 free previously unpublished Harlequin or Silhouette books and a postage and handling refund. For every specially marked book purchased during October, November and December, Harlequin/Silhouette will donate 5¢ to **Big Brothers/Big Sisters Programs and Services** in the United States and Canada for a maximum contribution of $100,000.00.